# The Moss Gatherers

## Matt Briggs

StringTown Press

The author would like to thank the editors of 5_Trope, The Northwest Review, The
Rendezvous Reader: A Manual of Northwest Literature, The Seattle Review, The
South Dakota Review and StringTown, where portions of this book initially appeared.
Additional thanks to The Seattle Review for awarding "Red Breast" the
Nelson Bentley Prize in Fiction.

Thanks, also, to Lisa Purdy, Polly Buckingham, Heath Herrick, and Jenny Heard for
their help with these stories.

Publication of this book is made possible in part by support from the Office of Arts &
Cultural Affairs, City of Seattle.

**Office of**
**ARTS &**
**CULTURAL AFFAIRS**

StringTown Press
P.O. Box 1406
Medical Lake, WA   99022-1406
stringtown@earthlink.net
home.earthlink.net/~stringtown

To Lisa

# The Moss Gatherers

JAQ HADN'T CALLED, but his sister didn't worry because he had once bicycled across the Hindu Kush where there weren't any phones and arrived back safely in France, sunburnt and with a string of odd new words he liked to say. He'd been in Chile, pedaling all of the way to the tip of South America, where he was robbed at machete point. The highwaymen didn't want any trouble. They just wanted his money. He knew how to take care of difficult situations, and so when she didn't hear from him during the summer, she didn't worry. How dangerous could America be, the American West? Not very dangerous, really. It was a built-up country. Despite the movies and the Associated Press which promised backwoods rapists, two men kidnapping a trail jogger and keeping her as their wife, two naked women escaping a backyard bunker in New Mexico where they'd been kept as sex slaves, the place couldn't really be that bad. Sensational news was a global epidemic. Jaq, though, was further west than New Mexico. Jaq was on the Pacific Coast, in Oregon. The name itself conjured to his sister in Grenoble a place beyond a place, some place too far to even think about.

When the cards stopped arriving, Melanie began to worry because Jaq had the habit of mailing a postcard every day so he could read them again when he returned. He transcribed them into his travel notebook. He wrote his trips up for a small magazine published in Paris. It didn't pay a thing, but this was how he recorded his trips.

The postcards, too, were a distillation of her brother. At home, he schemed and planned for his next trip. His time home was an interim time. He often said that every day he wasn't on the road was a day he was dead.

"You are here with me," Melanie had said.

"Oh yes. This is nice," he'd said. He only had one thing on his mind: how to get time and money to fund his next adventure. Once he was gone, the postcards carried with them all of his sense of humor. Melanie didn't mind because she received his postcards, and he wasn't underfoot. She could look forward to his return. She understood him through his cards. In Oregon, he wrote about following two gruff loggers down the street from the hostel where he was staying. They went into a diner and ordered black coffee and eggs and something called bloody beer. "For an instant I thought they had some blood in the refrigerator, some run off from the grill; they pour tomato juice and this hot sauce you can find everywhere in America—almost as common as catsup—Tabasco sauce? Bloody beer isn't as bad you'd think," he wrote.

The postcards made her excited to see him when he returned; however, on his return, the life that had been in his short notes disappeared. He was back to his distracted self. They kept house and depended on each other to keep things together. With him around, she didn't have to do anything about not having done anything with her life. She looked forward to his departure. She had done things. She'd been to school. She had her career at the hospital. She was an administrator. She never really did anything in the world aside from show up to work on time. The world itself with its erratic flow of events didn't even bother showing up on time. Sunset occurred when the light failed.

Their brother, Jason, who lived in Paris, had said to Melanie, "You have an office with a door. You don't punch a clock. You can afford a nice place."

"A nice place with my brother. That's almost as bad as living with our parents."

"Take it easy. Enjoy things," he had said. "Things happening is just stress. Who needs that?"

"I," Melanie had said, "need something to happen." The postcards from her brother were access to a life lived by someone. She suspected the same about Jaq as well, that he felt compelled to go on his trips, compelled to inject his postcards with a distillation of the travel, because his normal life as a teacher instructing fifteen year olds in computers would turn even the most durable Zen monk into a cardigan-wearing, crooked old man with a comb over. Together Jaq and Melanie were always waiting for his return or departure.

Nothing happened in her life with Jaq. This was what she wanted, she thought. Jaq in her life. Nothing could happen. This was how she wanted it. Although really she wanted Jaq to change, for him to listen to her when she talked about her day at the office, to take her out to the movies, to do more than pay for his half of the house cleaning bill. She wanted to spend a Sunday morning with him reading the newspaper and drinking coffee and making plans to visit a garden. She sometimes returned early from work just to see the cleaning woman finishing, so that she could see someone who was not her in the house. When Jaq was home, she hardly noticed he was home. He studied travel books and magazine and researched his trips on the Web. He was her brother, she reminded herself. He was supposed to feel free to do whatever he wanted to do; he had no obligations to her. She'd moved into the house expecting something different, and it hadn't happened. She didn't know what she expected. She couldn't think of it in the easy way other people would think about it because it wasn't easy like that. She didn't want Jaq to be a substitute boyfriend. Not that. Rather since he cared for her and since she cared for him, they could provide each other company.

After a few days, when a bundle of postcards didn't arrive, Melanie called Jason. Melanie had long, black hair and liked to wear white men's shirts and men's slacks and sandals. When he saw her, Jason asked her how The Pink Floyd had been at the theater. Jason had no trouble making a connection with his sister. Their ease together, paradoxically, meant they hardly saw each other. They sat in the living room drinking coffee and talking about Jaq and she wanted Jason to stay, but late in the afternoon, he shrugged and said it was late. He needed to get back. He kissed her on the cheek and gave her a hug.

After another week, Jason and Melanie regarded the absence of any contact from their brother with increasing alarm. Melanie shuffled and reshuffled the circulars and carefully paged through the catalogs in case a card had slipped among the glossy folds. Late one evening, the phone rang. A man said his name. She didn't write it down because he spoke quickly. He said his name as a formality, as a point of reference, and not something for the record. He did say slowly he was calling from Astoria in the State of Oregon in the Pacific Northwest of America. Jaq had been found stripped, beaten, his body flung into a creek near a closed state park about six miles from U.S. Highway 101, the highway he'd been bicycling around.

Jason slept in the house that night and in the morning he prepared for Melanie breakfast, baguette with strawberry jam, yogurt, and coffee. He asked her how she slept and she looked at him in his bathrobe and she felt almost happy for half a minute.

"I don't know how I feel," she said.

Melanie pictured the American West as a large flat place with mesas and cactus shaped like crosses with their arms curved at the end and cupped toward the blazingly hot sky. But when she and her brother exited the plane at Portland it was wet. While rain didn't fall, something moist settled out of the sky and coated the ground. The gutters flowed with the accumulated drizzle.

Jaq was dead. They didn't really believe this, thinking instead it was some kind of mistake, some kind of error, that really maybe some person had stolen his wallet and they had been killed and really he was somewhere else. He had always been so careful on his trips, and America was a real country like France. He hadn't even been shot. Or rather, the body, whoever it was, hadn't been shot. They arrived very late in Astoria. They couldn't sleep with the jet lag and the strangeness of the place because even though it was the American West it wasn't dry like a cinematic western, but damp like a gigantic, oppressive version of Germany or England; dripping thickets crowded the shoulders of the highway and overburdened logging trucks zipped past them showering the car with wood chips and gravel.

The next morning, they drank coffee and ate eggs at a diner. The city was busy with people going about their normal routines. It was a small town with big business. A fog horn bleated over the placid waves of the river. In the distance, they could see the arc of a bridge climbing over the huge river. The arc disappeared into the clouds of moisture. The Columbia was more of a sea really than just a river. Jaq had sung the song when he left, "Roll on, Columbia, roll on!"

After breakfast they met the sheriff at the morgue. He wore a polished, tin star on his pocket and led them down some wooden stairs. The steps creaked under them and sounded as though they would come apart. They were below the street level in a vault that was freezing, and there was their brother on a metal shelf in a sort of corpse filing cabinet.

Jaq didn't look alive, but he looked more alive then she had thought he would; that is, Melanie thought he would hardly be recognizable. She thought he would look the way they do in the movies—there was an effect, a look as though someone had put makeup on him to make him look dead—but at the same time there he was: his hair a little longer than when they had seen him a month ago, but otherwise he seemed clean and uninjured, just lying very still and holding his breath. Melanie leaned down.

"Is this Jaq Deloit?" the officer asked.

"It is him, isn't it?" Melanie asked her brother. Jason had tears coming out of his eyes and she wanted to cry too because they had not made a mistake; he had been killed out there in the wilderness they had just driven through.

"It is him," Jason said. They climbed the creaking stairs. It was too warm in the upstairs office. It smelled like coffee and body odor. The fluttering light from the overhead florescent made everything look like it had sunk, suddenly. The sheriff led them to a paper-stuffed office overlooking a busy downtown street with people sitting outside on white plastic chairs under an awning. Puddles collected in the street and made noise when cars drove over them. They filled out the paperwork. He handed them, finally, Jaq's effects.

"He was killed?"

"Yes."

"Who killed him?"

"We don't have a suspect. We think it was a moss gatherer."

"A what?"

"A transient. There are moss gatherers living in the forest. They earn what money they need by gathering moss. They can always find moss. In season, they also find mushrooms and ginseng. We think it might have been one of these people. It would have to have been someone without a car, because there were no tracks at the scene of the crime. Just your brother and his bicycle. He was camping and something happened."

"Don't you have a better idea than that?"

"He was a stranger here—he didn't know not to camp there. People around here know not to camp in the forest this time of year. The weather drives these people out of the backwoods."

"Why don't you do something?" Jason asked

"I've never seen one," he said. "I've just heard reports of them stealing chickens, breaking into people's homes to get food. Things like this. I don't recall anyone getting killed before. The perpetrator must have perceived that your brother was a stranger. I don't know."

"Have you looked?"

"We are following up on all of the pertinent leads," the sheriff said.

They went back to the hotel and made arrangements to have Jaq's body sent back to France.

The police wanted to keep the clothes Jaq had been wearing at the time of his death. His other clothes were folded and wrapped in plastic. They had examined these as well. Each one had a sticker and number and had been photographed and placed into their database. That is how the sheriff had explained it. "We have everything about the event stored now and if something comes up or if we uncover anything we will have a place to look for this information."

They had Jaq's rucksack as well. Jaq had been proud of the rucksack, because after he started using it, it became the official issue of the French-Swiss Search and Rescue Team. He carried everything he needed in it: a compact tool kit for repairing his bicycle, first aid kit, a lightweight, high mountain cooking and mess kit, and the pack of blank postcards he'd bought from gas stations and museums on Highway 101.

Melanie thought about the emptiness of the house. Even if she could afford it, would she want to be there by herself? Maybe Jason would move into it with her. The house would be paid off. Jason had a life in Paris, but Paris wasn't far away and the city he grew up in had its own charms. It was a charming city. It was a nice place to be. They went to a bar and drank.

She wanted to ask Jason, "So do you want to move in with me?" However, she didn't even know how to broach the subject.

Instead, she paged through the postcards. There was one that had been written and a stamp placed on it. "I ate my lunch in the spray of a mountain creek today. The creek was just off the highway, and I ate an orange and drank an orange soda I bought in a brown bottle from the Thriftway. The soda tastes more like orange than the orange. I will sleep outside tonight. Already it is getting dark and I can see the stars, but my guide says the sun doesn't set for another hour. Maybe it is the mountains that make it so dark here?"

The next day they started to drive back to the airport. There would be no more postcards.

Melanie would have a lot of money once she returned to France. Jaq and she each held an insurance policy. When they bought the house they had foresight enough to insure themselves in case one of them died. Melanie could pay off the house and have money left. She could go on a trip herself, a cruise in the Indian Ocean aboard a freighter surrounded by metal containers and a vast, starkly blue ocean. An adventure. Who knows where she would go? The sun visor in the rental car, a fuzzy flap, bothered her. She kept confusing the shadow at the edge of her field of vision for an insect. She swatted her temple. She pressed the visor back against the ceiling. She should not benefit from her brother's death. He was murdered. She imagined herself working day after day in the big, cool house, returning home to sit in the kitchen and read her junk mail. Her life was like this anyway, but at least she could always look forward to Jaq's return.

Jason smiled at her and rolled down the window to let the smell of the forest and river into the car. Rain whipped in and then he pressed the windows closed and they groaned and snapped shut. He even enjoyed driving back to the airport. He would be a pleasure to live with and the house was big. He could afford to live there because it would be paid for, now. She didn't know if he would leave Paris. When they returned, he'd probably go back to his apartment.

"What do you think a moss gatherer is like?" she asked.

"We have the poor in France, too," he said. "Maybe they are like Gypsies? I can't even imagine what they'd be like here. Everything seems so desperate already. Even that sheriff looked poor. There is either the town or nothing in Oregon."

"Where do they live? Maybe if we find one, they can give us clues about the one that killed him." Melanie didn't want to return to France to the house with Jaq's things in it. She couldn't imagine reporting to work in six weeks after her leave was up. She would get there on time.

"He's dead, Melanie. Aside from that, there is nothing else really to do."

"But whoever killed him shouldn't get away with it."

"Does it matter to us?"

"I just want to know what happened to him."

"It won't tell you anything. It'll be like one of his postcards. You can make sense of it, but it won't sound like Jaq."

"What do you mean?"

"It's just his postcards," Jason said, "were always such an act. He could have stayed at home and done just as well. Better maybe. It might have been more natural."

"You didn't like his postcards?"

"You liked his postcards? I didn't mean. I meant—"

"You said it," she said.

Jason parked at a viewpoint on the U.S.30. Sedans and sport utility vehicles raced up the steep slope past a bus. The air around them flowed quickly and smelled like the river and pine trees and the sea even though the Pacific was almost twenty miles away from here. Melanie could see over the steep bank of the Columbia where it cut into Oregon, over the distant plain alongside the Washington State side of the river, over dairy farms, and the beginning of foothills for a mountain range she didn't even know. The entire view would have been a substantial, ancient portion of France, a place where some things had happened. Here there was the possibility they'd come across the route of Lewis and Clark, or maybe an old English Fort, but the history of this place was buried under the conquest and settlement of it by the British and Americans. She was aware there were indigenous people who lived here still and had lived here all along, but standing at the viewpoint in the rush of air and the rattle of sedans straining up the hill and then finally the grumble of the bus as it eased up the grade past them, none of this really mattered. There was the new land, the fields and interstates, the gas stations and roadside diners, but there was under this, still, the old land, the land that Lewis and Clark must have first crossed. This wild place was a place she couldn't quite put her finger on because it was covered with so much contemporary refuse—this was the place their brother must have been drawn to. He talked about the raw beauty of the land. So far they had only seen clear cuts, quarries where the rock had been cut from the earth, a town built on fill and pilings that jutted far out into the water where it should not have been. At this point, she had only seen what the land looked like when business took control of it.

Jason shrugged. "I can't wait to get back home and leave this place behind."

"Don't you miss him?"

"I have missed him for a while," Jason said. "He didn't really like what I was up to. He didn't like how I lived my life."

"You'll just take off when we get back?"

"I'm sure we'll see each other more often," he said. "I'm sure we will."

"Can you stay at the house for a while?"

"How long?"

"A month? A month isn't a long time."

"It's ages."

"I don't know if I can go home yet," Melanie said.

"Don't end up waiting for Jaq to return," Jason said. "He's not going to."

"I know. He's not coming back," she said. She said this with a groan in the back of her throat. The words came out, each one by itself. "Every time I open the mail," she said, "I'll be expecting him."

"That's a song," Jason said.

"Are you making fun of me?"

He stood close to Melanie. "I'm sorry." She lay her head on his shoulder. "I thought we would find this was a mistake," he said.

"It is a mistake."

"I mean, that they had the wrong body."

"I did too."

Melanie noticed a faint trail leading from the vantage point along the side of the cliff. She climbed over the guard rail and stood on the narrow track. Jason stood on the other side and didn't move to follow her. Instead he took out his pack of cigarettes. The trail went between the shrubs and into a narrow cleft. She normally would not go down something like this. There was no sense in going down something like this; it would just take her to some dead end place. This was something that made her different than her brother Jaq. Why go somewhere when you only had to return again? She'd spent three years studying in Maryland. That had a sense to it, it was a program and it was located in the United States. But she found the entire concept of vacation a little bit foreign. What was the point in going somewhere if you just had to come back? Why go down this track if you just had to come back? Why go to America to bicycle in the wilderness if you were just going to get killed?

Melanie walked along the trail and passed under a gigantic rock with dripping water and into a stand of trees. Standing in the semidarkness it seemed she had come into the middle of the wilderness, just a step or two off the freeway, a seeming public, somewhat urban space, and now she stood among cedar trees and it smelled like cedar and the warm, packed odor of rotting vegetation. As her eyes adjusted to the pale light, she saw that the forest floor here was packed with garbage that had been tossed from the road. Among this garbage, she saw blood-soaked trousers or trousers soaked in something that looked like blood. It had dried now. There were stuffed animals matted with congealed fluid—garbage, who knows what it was. She pushed through the shrubs and found herself on a grassy knoll overlooking the view again. How could they find her brother in a place like this where so many things were already lost?

"I want to find him," she said.

"He's gone," Jason said.

"I want to find a moss man," she said.

On the road, Jason drove to the little town where Jaq had started his trip. Melanie paged through the record of where he'd been tracked in credit card charges. "Stop here," she said.

"No," Jason said.

"Stop," she said.

They booked a room at the same motel where Jaq had stayed his first night. Melanie asked the man at the front desk if he remembered a Frenchman who'd been there in the spring.

When Melanie said "Frenchman" in Oregon she thought of some Canadian fur trapper with a wool plaid shirt, suspenders, a raccoon cap. She didn't mean Jaq, gangly except for his overly thick, perpetually spandex clad thighs, his chest thin and narrow and almost completely oval like a tin flask. His Adams apple stood out from his body. He talked in a flowery, French-inflected English.

The man at the desk shook his head. "We get all kinds," he said. "Everyone runs together after awhile."

The next morning at the café where Jaq had charged eight dollars and thirty-seven cents, she and Jason sat at the window and looked out over the broken sidewalk. A white and yellow weed grew up between the cracked cement. They drank the local coffee; they'd lost hope of finding fresh roasted grounds in the Oregon countryside. The coffee was bad but it had an acidic quality they liked. It was what everyone else in the café drank. The dining room smelled like fried eggs and the coffee burner and something else she couldn't put her finger on. Jaq had been in this room for breakfast. She checked out the menu and couldn't reconstruct what he'd had.

"How many waitresses work here?"

The waitress was a thin, young woman who spoke with a deep, matronly voice, charred and raspy. Her brown hair had a little gray in it. She wore it tied behind her head with a black ribbon. She wore thick, functional shoes. She wore a single-piece uniform coated with old stains washed into the fabric and new stains beginning to set. "I'm the day waitress," she said.

"Were you here on September 20TH?"

"I'm always here," she said. "Day-in and day-out."

"Do you remember a bicyclist that day?"

"I don't even remember what day of the week September 20TH

was," she said. "I'm not going to remember a single customer."

She looked around. "I know who is a good tipper and who likes their coffee full. That's about it. You come in here five or six times, I'll remember you."

"He was," Melanie said, "a Frenchman."

"A what?"

"He was from France."

"How would I know where he's from? I'm from Austin."

"He had French accent."

"I don't know. What does a real French accent sound like?"

"I have one," Jason said.

"I can't hear it. Say something."

"We are tracking down my brother's last steps. He was killed in October on Highway 101. He was here ten days before his death. He spent $8.37 at breakfast time. We don't even know what the weather was like that day."

"What did he look like?"

"Skinny. Wearing spandex. He had a French accent."

"I think I do. He drank a bloody beer."

"He did?" Jason asked. "What is that?"

"Beer with V8 and Tabasco."

"Can we have two?" Melanie asked.

"Miller?"

"Whatever he had, we want that too."

"I don't want one," Jason said.

When the waitress left, Melanie leaned across the table. "Why don't you want to try it? Have a bloody beer with me."

"I am not interested in this."

"You can be cold," she said.

"Drink one with him alone."

"He's dead," she said, "if you haven't noticed."

The waitress gave Melanie a brown bottle, a little red bottle of Tabasco sauce, and a shot of red vegetable juice.

"What do I do?"

"You haven't had this?"

"No."

"Hangover cure."

Melanie drank the beer. It was spicy and watery.

"It would have been sunny," Jason said. "You have to remember that."

When the waitress came back Melanie asked her, "Do you know what a moss gatherer is?"

"I've heard of them."

"Do you know where we can find one?"

"Not a clue," she said. "I'm not sure what they are."

They were at a gas station when the attendant came to the pump. He was a young man with a thin mustache. "Do you know what a moss gatherer is?" Melanie asked him.

The man looked around and then he looked at Melanie and Jason and shrugged. "What is it?"

The rain let up and a greenish sky began to break through the clouds. They parked at the edge of a vast clear-cut that went on for seemingly hundreds of miles. They had heard of such things, of the rain forest in Brazil getting cut down. But they only imagined small areas cut down. The entire landscape here had been cut down, every vertical stick turned horizontal, over ridges, over mountains, streams, lakes; it was just a vast field of broken limbs, dirt, and tractor marks. It exposed the land underneath, rocky ridges, swampy depressions, tiny hills that would have disappeared under the lush, hundreds of feet of carpet provided by the forest. In this space, they were painfully aware of what wasn't there. The forest was gone and there were just huge puffy clouds.

"Do you think," Melanie asked, "that they made it up?"

"What do you think they made up?"

"The moss man."

"Why would they make that up?"

"They had to find something to blame his death on. Someone had to have killed Jaq because he was dead. It sounds sort of like the village monster to me. The moss man got your brother."

"'He was an outsider,' that's what the sheriff said."

"Do you think they know who did it?"

"I don't think so. I don't think they really care. They can chalk it up to a freak occurrence. As long as they can convince themselves it won't happen again."

"We should just go home," Melanie said. "He's gone. I don't even know what we are looking for. What if we find one? What if we even find the man that killed him?"

"Don't you want to see?"

"See what? There is nothing to see. There is nothing here. We need to go home. I always thought that sometime I'd get a postcard from Jaq and it would be like a key and I would understand him. That it would come and I would read it and when he returned, he'd be like I knew he was, instead of the way he was, if that makes any sense."

"He was never going to change," Jason said. "You knew that. That's what you were counting on."

At dusk, they passed through the small town near the campground where Jaq'd been killed. "Let's get a room," Melanie said. "This is a waste of time. We are just prolonging his death instead of getting over it."

"Where do you want to eat?"

"I don't want to eat another hamburger," Melanie said.

They stopped at the Thriftway. Jaq had spent twenty-three dollars there on the day of his murder. She put the thought out of her mind. They got green beans and lamb chops and found reasonable coffee and cream. At the check-out Melanie almost resisted asking if they'd remembered a Frenchman. They didn't.

That night, they found a room with a kitchen and prepared the meal. After eating, they put on their jackets and took their mugs of coffee out into the dripping outdoors and walked down the block to a little park. There was a swing set, rubber seats, a slide with water rolling down it. They drank their coffee and smoked Lucky Strikes. This was Jason's cigarette in America. She realized sitting in the dark that she was enjoying herself. She knew she should feel guilty about it. She was here because of her brother's grisly death. In any case, though, this was a place where she would never have come and it was unlike any place in France. The coarse, bloated grass grew in clay-packed soil. She had felt that everywhere in the world was becoming the same place. But they didn't have these tall, scraggly trees with their long, arced limbs, drooping bushy boughs and dripping water in France.

When they finished the cigarettes, Jason offered her another one. They blew the smoke up into the darkness. She watched the tiny drops float down from way above them, down into the light, and then onto the grass where it turned into a tiny bead. Eventually the beads, after they had smoked another cigarette and she started to feel sick and a little high, clumped together into a drop and rolled down the blade.

"We could buy some moss," Melanie said.

"You have to come to terms with his death."

"What about you?" she asked him. "You seem like a rock of acceptance. Doesn't Jaq's death bother you?"

"That sounds like Jaq," Jason said. "His death more than bothers me. But I just let this kind of thing wash over me and sort it out later. You're the one who is all busy trying to make sense of it. How can sense be made of it? Do you want to get it out of the way so it doesn't come back to bother your later when you're at a coffee break at the hospital?"

"We could buy some moss at a nursery," she said. "They might know."

"Did you hear what I said?"

"I'm letting it wash over me so I have something to do during my coffee break at the hospital."

They went back to their room and before she closed the door she looked at the mountains just beyond the trees. In the night there was just the steady hush as drizzle settled on the trees and dripped to the forest floor. She could see the black bulk of the hills under the faintly brown clouds. In there, somewhere, lived the moss man that had maybe killed their brother. When someone killed someone it was said they claimed their life. In which case, Melanie wanted it returned.

"We are buyers from France," she told Jason.

"I'm not going."

"Just go with me to the nursery."

"And then?"

"We can do what you want to do."

The nursery had been built around an old farm. The barn sagged in the middle like an old cardboard box. Melanie thought the barn would be red, but instead it was grey and brown, covered with patches of moss. The nursery itself was run out of the farmhouse that had been converted into offices and surrounded by posts and lintel yards covered with fiberglass.

They found a rock garden with pallets of moss.

"Where can I find a supply of moss? More moss than this?"

"We can order it for you."

"I'm writing an article about moss for *Garden Today*," she said. "Of course I'll mention your wonderful place."

"You might try Linda Hartwell's Landscaping Supply. It's

between here and Astoria."

In the car, Jason said, "Okay, I want to go to the airport. Back to *Garden Today*'s corporate offices."

Melanie didn't say anything. Jason drove anyway to the Landscape Supply place off the highway. It was a warehouse built under the cliffs of an abandoned quarry. Heaps of stones lay on the drive up. A man in a hardhat with bright orange plugs coming out of his ears walked briskly over to their car and tapped on the window. "We only sell to the trade."

"We are looking for moss," Melanie said.

"You've got a contractor card?"

"We are from France," Jason said, playing up his accent. "We are buyers and tracked down the supply of moss here."

"It is good moss," the man said. "Best moss in the world is from the Pacific Coast. People used to use the moss to dress bandages. Before gauze. Now they just use it for their yards. Bill Gates has our moss. Corporate offices all around the world have our moss. You came to the right place."

"We are preparing a shipment of moss samples to France," Melanie said, playing up her accent.

"You want more? How about tomorrow?"

"Tomorrow. That sounds great. We were just about on our way back to France. We may want to set up regular shipments at some point before we head back to Grenoble."

They staked out the supply place and a rattletrap truck came the next morning with pallets wrapped in white plastic. After a man unloaded the truck, they followed it. The truck drove for many miles on the highway, and then turned onto a narrow, single lane gravel road. Their car began to shake in the pot holes. The truck barreled along at an impossible speed and they kept behind it. Jason was having trouble with the turns. "He's familiar with the road. I don't know if I can keep up with him," and then after a little bit, the truck was gone.

"We've lost him," he said. They drove along the road and then saw the truck on the other side of the river parked at a trailer. They drove up and then back and couldn't figure out how to get across.

"What are we going to do?"

"Talk to him about the moss man. Maybe he is one."

"But what if he is? He's right here."

There was a log that went out into a gravel bar in the middle of the river. From the gravel she could hop onto the top of a rock and get onto the shore. The log was very slippery. At the very end of it she slipped off. Her shoes just lost it and she landed on the gravel. The river was so clear it was just a flow of loose leaves, a faint green waving distortion down to the gravel bottom. She kicked gravel into the river. Jason came behind her and gingerly stepped off the log. They hopped on top of the rocks onto the muddy bank of the river and climbed up to the yard.

They could hear music coming from inside the trailer. A thick, industrial churning sound. They knocked on the door. Nothing. They banged on the door. Nothing. They went to a window and looked in and the man looked up from the counter where he was making a sandwich. He had a short goatee with grey in it. He had hardly any hair on his head, and what hair he did have looked like stubble. He wore a T-shirt with holes in it. Melvins. And under that he wore red longjohns. He looked at them and then came to the door with his hand on something he held behind the door. "I don't buy things from people coming to my door," he said.

He looked around at his truck. "How'd you all get here?"

"We don't—"

"What you are doing is trespassing and in this state I am within my rights to shoot you."

"We are looking for a moss gatherer," Melanie said.

"That *War-shh-ington* State accent has become strong."

"We are French."

He stared at them.

"From France?" Jason said.

"Of course," he said. "You are French from France. That explains it. That tells me a whole fucking lot."

"Do you know where we can find a moss gatherer?"

"Yes," he said. "But I can't. I mean I could if I knew where one was but I don't know where one is. They are out there somewhere."

"Oh," she said. "We're looking for one."

"I see," he said. He nodded his head and looked at her and then glanced at Jason. "Come in, I guess," he said. "I'm way out here. I can't be too careful. Bruce." He offered his hand.

"How do you do Bruce," Melanie said. She introduced herself and her brother. He looked at them and nodded his head and cocked it to one side as though he were settling the information into a slot.

"Melanie and Jason, can I get you something to drink? Beer? Coffee. The coffee is cold but I could nuke it. I've got 2%."

"I'm all right. Thank you," Melanie said.

"A beer would be good," Jason said.

The man took a can from the half-case on the counter. He tossed it to Jason. Jason dropped it.

"Damn," the man said. "Frenchmen from France don't know how to catch beer? Rule One: don't let it drop." He tossed another one.

Jason caught it.

"How did you arrive at my doorstep?"

"My brother was killed by a moss man. We decided to track one down, so we went to a nursery, the wholesaler, the supplier—you."

He shook his head. "I have to be more careful in the future.

You know I remember that thing. Happened just a couple weeks back. They didn't say anything about who they thought did it. Who thinks a moss man did it?"

"Sheriff we talked to said he thought they did."

"Does he know where you are?"

"We are meeting him in town tomorrow morning, first thing," Melanie said.

"Oh yeah," Jason said. "We have an appointment with the sheriff tomorrow."

"Moss men don't kill people. They're just getting by; they just do what they got to do to make it. They live out here and scrape along. You want to live in a ditch? You want to sleep in a lean-to made of twigs? That's how they live. They live like that and so people blame them for whatever. What would they kill him with? Most of them don't even have teeth."

"He was strangled."

"I don't have the fucking answers to your brother's death," the man said. "But I seriously doubt a moss man would be strong enough to kill a sheep. They get blamed for that all the time, too." He drank his beer down to the bottom and crushed it flat with a sudden blow on the counter top. "So what if you find a moss man?"

"I don't know," Melanie said.

"A moss man is just an excuse for the cops. The moss man killed him. That way he doesn't have to track down the killer. If it'd been some local guy, no family would take that. 'Then find the fucking moss man,' they'd tell the cops because they know these guys aren't dangerous. I'm sorry about your brother. People dying sucks shit, but people getting killed, that just doesn't have to happen."

"I just want to see a moss man."

"There is nothing to see," he said. "There is nothing to see at all."

"How do you get your moss?"

"You want to play me that way," he said. "Okay. I'll show you. You want to see how I do this deal? Let's go get a load of moss. Get ready for the damn moss man." Bruce put on his boots. He looked at their shoes and then chuckled. "Those things are going to get totaled. Don't you have some boots or something?"

"This is it," Jason asked.

"We're going," Melanie said.

Bruce led them out under the trees. He carried a black plastic bag over his shoulder like a backwoods Santa Claus. They walked up a steep muddy slope. Jason used a branch to climb the worst parts. Mud and leaves coated their shoes, their ankles, all of the way up to their butts. At the top of a steep climb, Jason turned around and the ground came loose under him and he started to slide. "Help!" he called and Melanie grabbed him and then he almost pulled her down with him. They started to laugh and Bruce stood at the top of the slope. He took out his pack of cigarettes, and then they all stood at the very top looking out over the forest.

They could see the trailer's plume of smoke.

When they finished, Bruce held up the butt. "This drove them away. They can smell something like this on our breath."

"Why did you smoke, then?" Melanie asked.

"If you think the smell of smoke driving them away is bad, what do you think two Frenchies rolling down a muddy bank is going to do?"

"You could have told us."

"I told you, I don't see them. I made my arrangements and this is it. This is how I meet them."

They came into a clearing at the top of the hill. It was surrounded by maple trees. Red and gold leaves covered the forest floor. Under the tree there was a load of moss. Bruce took the moss and replaced the garbage sack full of potatoes, a packet of jerky, and a half-case of beer. "This is it," he said. "We can wait, but they aren't going to come out until we're gone."

They left and went down to the trailer and drank a few more beers. Bruce played them a record. He said, "I'm sorry to hear about your brother."

"Are you coming with us?" Melanie asked.

"No need," Bruce said.

The sun didn't set at dusk in a final shutting off of light. Gradually the overcast light dissipated. The darkness that had been under the sword ferns and beneath the thickets of fir seeped out. Along the river the cold air smelled of water-roiled sediment. As they climbed the muddy slope again, Melanie and Jason were careful to place their weight on solid undisturbed areas. They tested their steps. The last of the daylight glanced against the silver trunks of the maple trees in the clearing. Melanie half expected to see someone there. She thought she heard someone there, listening for a crack of a branch, an exhalation of breath, a half-uttered hello. The forest moved. Limbs rattled together. Needles on fir boughs rolled. Stray red maple leaves fluttered through the empty space and back into the forest. The groceries were gone. Melanie leaned down by the tree to see if she could find something, some sign: the tread of a boot, an impression of a knee, anything. There was nothing aside from the moss and a snail hiding in its bark colored shell.

On the way back down the slope, she found she wasn't thinking now about tracking the moss man down. The moss man didn't know about her brother. She was certain then that no one except the person who had killed him knew what had happened. They wouldn't be able to explain Jaq's absence. They could merely explain just how they had killed him. It had happened. She found, as she walked down the slope, that she no longer questioned it. She had been thinking all along that maybe if she could somehow find more information she could understand and maybe undo the event. Although Jason walked in front her, he wouldn't let her use his shoulder as balance. "I'm falling," she said and he stood aside to let her fall. It didn't hurt, but she was covered in earthy, slick muck by the time they got back down to the trailer. Bruce stood under the awning of his trailer with coffee for them.

"See anything?" he said.

"Nothing to see," Melanie said.

On the drive back to the motel she thought she might take a trip. Why return to a big empty house? She would send postcards she thought, but she wouldn't write anything on them to Jason. Maybe, "I miss you," or "Wish you were here," something that was true in any case.

# Inheritance

THE FATHER AND HIS SON went into the Cascade Mountains on a hike. They hadn't seen each other in a long time. Water still dripped out of the cedar trees, and the sunlight glanced off the puddles of water lying where puddles normally didn't lie. This was the first clear day in a long time.

In the long ago springs, the father and son used to hike often. They sometimes ran into hermits. When they came upon a hermit, it was always in the late spring, like now, when the snow had just started to melt from the highlands. The hermits migrated up from the valley floors, then, to buy Spaghetti Os and instant coffee at Truck Town on the interstate, and to prepare for the high country to open up.

Even though his son was his only child, the father was not close to him. The father had never lived with his son's mother. After his child was born, the father went into the mountains. When he returned, his son's mother had married another man. But the father argued with the mother about his rights to raise his son. The father was able to keep his son during the summer. His son remembered those summers fondly, but also with a little dread because he had to sleep on the hardwood living room floor in an old sleeping bag. The father didn't have a soft place to sit in his house. He didn't even have a sofa. His son spent all summer working at the father's house, mowing the lawn, cutting down the blackberries, although when the father wasn't working in the factory, they would go on long hiking trips.

Soon enough, his son wasn't a boy, but a young man with a wife. The son was looking to buy his first home. He asked his father for help with the down payment. He asked him in the city where they sometimes met to drink black coffee. The father and son sat under a coffee shop awning on the sidewalk near a busy street. Whenever a bus or truck roared down the street, the father jumped. The father said, "I can afford to help you, son. I could buy that house without blinking. But I will not be responsible for creating yet another weak and dependent excuse for a man. World is stocked with enough of them anyway." The father told his son, yet again, the story about how the father had been born on the railroad tracks in Idaho and from there he had forged his own way in life with his own sweat and endurance. As a result of this meeting, the son didn't see his father for many years. Sometimes the father called and told his son about the coldness in the mountains. The father told him about the sound of granite breaking free from the cliffs and the crash of the stone tumbling down the mountain. One day the father called and heard a baby talking in the background. "Put that kid on the phone." When the father heard his grandson, already five years old and talking and asking questions about the old man, the father burst into tears. "The child is so old. I have missed so much." The father saw his son and his grandson as a steady accumulation of life that stacked up, one prefix pushed onto the next, eventually pushing the father away from father, to grand-father, and finally to his death.

His son, at first out of pity for his father, began to see him. But the pity gradually wore away as the father refused his son's help to clean up his house and to mow his lawn. They started to go hiking again, once a month. Usually it rained, and they would hike along the muddy trails, coating the backs of their knees with filth. That day, though, when the father and his son went into the Cascade Mountains on a hike, it was clear and they could see for a long way down to the interstate, which crossed the Cascades at the lowest pass.

His son fell down a lot on the trail and had to jog to catch up with the father. The father was a stubborn old goat, with stout legs and knees like burls of an old cherry tree. The father was pretty clumsy as well. He sometimes looked back to see if his son had caught up, and then the father would trip. His son would rush up and try to help the father, but the father angrily brushed his son away. The father wasn't embarrassed by falling, he was embarrassed by his son's attempts to pick him up. "I can get up myself. If I was out here alone I wouldn't expect you to drive out here and pick me up."

"But I'm right here, Dad."

The father cursed. "Leave me alone, dammit."

After some time, the father started to enjoy his falls. He rolled on the ground and laughed. "You'll get your inheritance sooner than you think!"

There was a little snow where they were now, and they kept plunging through weak spots. They could walk for a long distance on the crusted snow. Under the snow they could hear the rush of the snow melt. When either one of them stepped down, they ran the risk of plunging through the snow all the way down until they hit something. Sometimes, they passed over places where there was no end. The bank went down into a canyon with a creek running way down in the darkness, or the snow heaped up at the edge of a long snow chute. The melting avalanches had cleared all the branches away from the scooped bottom of these chutes. The long snow chutes bothered the son the most because if the father or his son slipped down one of them, the body would accelerate until it would be impossible to stop. The son pictured himself stumbling into one and then shooting down the side of the mountain to his death. He became really cautious when he came to the chutes and so began to fall down even more because he didn't have the careless, forward momentum he needed to keep up on the snow. The father bounded across them and would stumble, or his leg would find a weak spot in the snow, and he would end up buried to his crotch, cackling.

After they had crossed a long stretch of ice chutes and the father even admitted that perhaps they should have brought snow shoes, they went down to a lake basin that was free of snow. After the ice and snow chutes, the mossy banks of the lake felt like the tropics. A hermit had set up camp there. He had a bedraggled beard and matted hair. He burned incense from a punk stuck into a fir tree and stood outside his tent. As he came down from his campsite, he nodded his head, but he didn't open his mouth. He stood about fifteen yards away from the father and son. He looked at them and blinked. His wool sweater unraveled around a hole in the starved apex of one elbow. Finally, he smiled at them.

"Nice weather up here," the father said.

"I slept on ice last night," the hermit said. His eyebrows were bushy and untrimmed.

"This is a regular hermit convention," the father said. The hermit didn't get the joke. The father didn't try to explain it to the hermit. Even though the son didn't get the joke either, he laughed, but a hoarse, fake laugh that startled the hermit. The hermit went back into his tent and closed the flap.

The father and his son crossed the lake basin and began to climb the mountain again. They continued to fall. The father laughed when his legs plunged through the snow, while his son cursed and sometimes asked the father to help him up. Instead of helping his son up, the father stood a short distance away and continued to laugh.

While they hiked, they talked about the hermit, and then they began to talk about the father's dream of self-sufficiency. "Don't you find any security that I am here to help you, Dad?"

The father had a fantasy he frequently discussed with his son. He wanted to come up to the mountains to live, to just camp and swim in the Alpine Lakes. In the father's fantasy it is perpetually August and hot, and he walks through a forest of silver fir trees under a big rock face covered with lichen. He comes through all of that bright blue and green wood out into the basin of the lake. The lake is deep and dark under the steep cliffs that plunge way down from the mountain tops into water so clear it's just a distortion of light and not a color.

They passed up onto a side of the mountain where the real, gigantic avalanches had happened. Rushing snow had shattered the trunks of ancient Douglas fir trees, leaving behind yellow splinters and the sweet odor of cracked lumber. They could see way down a chute. The father slipped and his son didn't reach down to help the father. The father giggled and rolled about four feet and then he stopped, as if by magic, of his own accord. His son grabbed a branch and leaned down to help the father and decided better of it. The father got to his feet and then slipped backward and shot down the slope. His son watched the figure of the father to see if the father managed to get a hold of anything, but the father got smaller, from the size of a fist to a thumb to a pinkie finger nail to nothing at all.

# Red Breast

OUR FRONT DOOR RATTLED, then a force shook our house, clinking the plates in the oak cabinet in the dining nook. I shook my husband, Jeff, but he didn't budge. He rolled over and started to snore. I poked him in the neck with my fingers until he turned his head and stopped snoring, but he didn't wake up. I waited and didn't hear anything for a long time. I listened to Jeff sleep. Maybe I had imagined the noise, or maybe a truck had driven by the house shaking everything. I was awake. I listened for anything outside, for anyone inside the house. I imagined I heard someone walking up the steps, breathing heavily, but then I realized it was just my heart going nuts and me working myself up into a fit. I looked at Jeff roaring along. He was content. He had a hard, round belly he wore like a prize. When he scooped me up to kiss me, I would inhale his sugary aftershave and his whiskers would scrape my cheeks. He woke me sometimes in the middle of the night with the onion odor of his flatulence or the idling engine groan of his deep, buzzing snore. I always fidgeted with the sheets before I fell asleep. Sometimes, I would turn onto my left side and hold my breath so that my ears would fill with blood and I couldn't hear anything for three or four seconds. Finally, I would give up and listen to Jeff fully satisfied, snoring, and asleep.

Something struck the front door and I was awake this time and it was unmistakable. I put on my silk nightgown and put my hand over Jeff's mouth and plugged his nose with a pinch. I felt his hot breath on my palm and then he jumped awake. "There's something outside trying to get in," I told him. He sat up in bed. His eyes were glass. "Go downstairs and find out what it is."

"I'm sleeping," he said. A noise came from the front of the house, not the solid thud that had woken me the first time, but an unmistakable object hitting the front door. The metal door rang faintly.

We didn't turn on any lights and reveal ourselves to the intruder. Jeff kept our handgun in a locked plastic case in a cardboard box underneath the bed. It was at times like this that I told him we needed to put that gun in a safe place, yes, but that gun needed to be where we could get our hands on it at a moment's notice. A person needs to feel safe in their own home. "Are you going to get the gun?" I asked, and he shook his head and walked clumsily down the hallway and down the steps, a rumbling *thud thud thud.* I surprised myself with how quietly I navigated down the hallway past my son Martin's bedroom, down the long stairs not missing a step, all of the way down into the entry hall under my chandelier, behind Jeff. The first light of day faintly fell through the two-story window where it caught the tall, sparkling shape of the cut glass. Odd to think there was an intruder just beyond the seeming peacefulness of our entryway.

Jeff came back from the kitchen and stood right under the chandelier. "There's no one inside here."

Outside, under the rising sun, under the distant peaks of the Cascade Mountains, our yard was dark. The streetlights had turned off.

"Why are the street lights off?" I whispered.

"They're tripped by solar cells," Jeff said. He explained ultraviolet light to me as light that the human eye can't see. To the human eye, the flood of ultraviolet light at dawn still seemed dark.

"What do you mean light we can't see? Invisible light is an oxymoron."

Jeff chuckled his superior chuckle. "Exactly, Lori."

Invisible light or not, I couldn't see. I heard the sound again at the front door, a rattle and then a knock and I just about dove into the coat closet. The front door shook. I looked through the blinds, just pulling apart the strands of aluminum a quarter of an inch to examine the front door. I didn't notice anything, it was so dark. And then something throbbed into the front window. "Jeff!" I hollered because some psychopathic, dysfunctional sociopath, some fancy, liberal-bent cluster of psychobabble (short for nut), was trying to force his deranged body into my house and then into me. The front door shook again. It rattled like someone about to kick down the door. They'd given it two good trial whacks and now had saved up the resolve to smash the hinges open. "Somebody is trying to get into the house," I said. "But I don't see anything."

The front door beat and shook for what seemed like a full minute. "Get down," Jeff whispered.

"I'm going to get the gun," I said.

Jeff rooted around in the coat closet where we kept our sports equipment and grabbed his ice pick; the front door shook again and then Jeff rushed the door. He threw it open and raised the ice pick up and the long, sharp heat-tempered point gleamed in the ultraviolet light.

An immense robin red breast, obviously stunned, sat on the *Welcome* mat, his huge heart-shaped chest as round as a bright, cherry-red jaw breaker. His black eyes reflected the light like two steel ball bearings. The bird shook itself, sending all of these spheres into gyrations and then cocked its head at Jeff. The cool early morning air flowed into our temperature-modulated home. I glanced around the front yard trying to see if the actual intruder—it couldn't be a bird, I thought—hid in one of the rhododendrons or beyond the fir tree. Our yard was as new and spare as a miniature golf course; the intruder didn't have anywhere to go in the instant that it took for Jeff to open the front door. The bird hopped toward Jeff and past us into the house. Jeff tried to knock the bird away with the ice pick and knocked out one of the panes of glass at the foot of the entryway. The bird flew into our front hall, up into my chandelier, and perched on one of the cross bars toward the top. The rising sunlight caught the cut glass and showered the foyer in cascades of glittering sparks and spectrums. The bird made a single peep.

"Is that bird the one making the noise?" Martin rubbed his eyes at the top of the stairs.

"Yes, honey," I said. "Isn't it extraordinary?"

My special project that spring was Warren Cornell's lost soul. I visited him on Friday and Saturday, evenings my family was usually very busy, so I wasn't missed. I drove out to the Monroe Correctional Facility right after supper to visit Warren, the youngest son of a very old, wealthy Seattle family. Warren stood accused of stalking and molesting fourteen young boys over a three-year period. This sounds common enough, I suppose, from the national section of the daily paper, which has endless sordid tales like Warren's story. However, Warren was someone I knew and these boys he had abused were all boys my son had played alongside of on soccer teams. I had spent long days at Jamborees with their mothers, cutting up orange slices and yelling in the drizzle in our bright Eddie Bauer yellow fisherman's raincoats.

Warren, as the accusation went, had carefully arranged his

volunteer work so that he would be surrounded by young boys—most of them leaving the safe world of their private elementary schools around the city for the rigorous, hormone-laden hallways of Bishop High—difficult times, I think for just about anybody. Warren confided in these boys and they in turn confided in him. My own son, Martin, belonged to the circle of friends that Warren mentored. I knew many of the boys who had accused Warren of these crimes. It was difficult for me take the easy road of righteousness and hate Warren for what he had done. Even though we all went to the same church, the parents were angry enough about what had happened to their children that I think they had forgotten how to be good Christians.

I grilled Martin about Warren Cornell and the boys that clung to him. I believed it was possible my son was involved in these crimes because we all do things, especially in those blank years after grade school and before we get out of college, long awkward years when we don't even find church interesting and we are strangers even to ourselves. Martin and I may have had an unnaturally communicative relationship for a mother and a fourteen-year-old son, but there are limits, and he refused to tell me everything. This didn't reassure me much about Martin. Martin was, to be honest, a bit odd. I don't mind saying so. Martin wore a red parka. He was fussy and instead of laughing, his face got squirrelly and he made a hacking noise. He had a single eyebrow—a wide patch of wiry hair over the bridge of his nose—up until three months ago. Jeff and I took him out for pizza to straighten him out.

I once found Martin on the street when I came home early. At first I saw the loose sheets of notebook paper and then school books scattered on the sidewalk. In our cul-de-sac a swarm of boys in their Bishop High uniforms had Martin cornered on the steps. Martin's face looked all blown up and red. His single hairy gash of an eyebrow arced over his nose. I parked in the middle of the boys and they sauntered away. I pulled Martin kicking and screaming inside the house. "Why are those boys picking on you?" He just sat on the couch. "What did you do?"

"I didn't do anything, Mom," he said. "I just don't belong."

I made him join soccer after that. Martin takes for granted the things that I've worked hard for him to have. He has opportunities handed to him I never even had a chance at, with my parents so poor I had to drop out of college just to help with the rent. Martin's classes are full of future CEOs, corporate lawyers, judges, and senators. The college recruiters take the guidance counselors out to lunch. But Martin has refused to cultivate lasting friendships with his classmates. If I hadn't put my foot down and forced him to join soccer, there would've been no telling how isolated he would be.

Jeff and I talked to Martin over pizza about the things that parents should talk to their son about in this day and age. If he was going to have sex, he was going to use a condom, even though I don't approve of boys his age having sex. I told him he would spend the rest of his life working at Dairy Queen if he did get a girl pregnant at his age. "We know we're not always there to make sure you're all right and doing what a good kid needs to do. God is present, but he isn't in the habit of slapping you on the side of the head when you're stupid. Use a condom. God knows where the tramps who'd put out at your age have been, anyway. A couple of young whores always hang out with the boys on the team. You're an athlete and it's likely those girls have already made themselves known to you. Thank the Lord, Martin, that you have a single eyebrow and insist on wearing that red parka."

Jeff touched my arm. "Lori," he said. He cleared his throat and turned to Martin. "Your mom is just worried about you. Don't listen to her. Listen to me. Don't you think it's time you did something about your eyebrow? You're a handsome kid and getting to that age where you'll have to start shaving and putting on cologne. You know, *grooming yourself.*"

"This is how I am. My friends like me the way I am."

"But we get older," Jeff said, "and we change. And that comes with some responsibilities, and we may not always like what we have to do."

We left it at that. I stood up and bought a pack of Camel Lights from the cigarette machine next to the arcade game—both of them had worn, chrome coin slots. The cellophane-wrapped package ticked into the metal tray. "Lori?" Jeff said, because I had quit a long time ago. But when my nerves fray, I smoke. I stood on the patio the Pizza Hut used in the summer; now in the early spring, the plastic tables were stacked in one corner, and a tarp covered them and water had pooled in the folds. Schools of mosquito larva swam around and around the brackish water. It's odd to me how life can live in a place just like that and even thrive in other people's neglect.

Martin opened the door and stood on the railing looking down into the damp patch of beauty bark and spindly evergreen trees lashed to long rods to keep them standing upright. "Mom? Is everything all right?"

"Do you think you can speak to me honestly, Martin?"

"I don't lie," Martin said.

"You are my son and I have long valued how I could ask you anything, no matter what, and you would speak to me as honestly as I speak to myself. I think we communicate well."

"Sure, Mom."

"Did Warren Cornell touch you?"

"No. Is that what you want to know?"

"Because if you are gay, Martin, we can get you some help."

I blew out a cloud of smoke and studied my son for a reaction to my question. But he just had a blank look on his face as though my question was completely meaningless. "Are you a homosexual?"

"I know what gay is, Mom." He shook his head as if he was tired. My little boy shook his head like a fifty-year-old overworked business man and went back inside.

When I went back inside, Jeff said, "Are you calmed down now?"

"Give me more of that pizza. I'm ravenous."

However, they had consumed the pizza. A bread stick lay in the coagulated marinara sauce. Jeff nervously looked at the aluminum pizza tray. He shrugged.

We finally forced the robin out of the open kitchen window. But it came back the next morning, flinging itself against the front door, against the front window, against the outside walls. Coming home from work in the daylight, I found feathers lodged into the siding and bird droppings on the front stoop. The robin woke me, banging on the front window at four o'clock in the morning. I walked downstairs and fixed a pot of coffee and sat at the kitchen table watching the day arrive.

I realized then that Martin was already sitting on the couch in the living room. "Hi, Mom," he said.

"What are you doing down here? It's four o'clock in the morning."

"I was waiting up for the robin," Martin said. "What do you think it wants? Maybe this house stands where its ancestral tree used to grow. It's just trying to get home."

"It doesn't want anything, honey, it's a crazy bird. And if it keeps up this noise, it will be a crazy, dead bird." But I was sorry as soon as I said that because Martin scowled and then went back upstairs without saying anything to me.

Warren Cornell drove a hunter green Volvo. He wore oversized sweaters. He was athletic. He was thin. He had wispy brown hair, always a little blond from the time he spent on the soccer field. He had sharp features and very red, thin lips. I think all the mothers were a little in awe of him because he could talk to us about our decorating and the good sales at little hidden neighborhood home decorating stores, and he could talk to our husbands about sports and Microsoft, the two things that the men wanted to talk about, and he knew how to balance all of these conversations at once. He volunteered as assistant coach for soccer. He was a clean, wholesome young man, whom everyone took to be a little directionless because he was waiting to take a position in his father's company and, until then, he spent his time volunteering at the Lake Washington Presbyterian Church and coaching soccer.

When I visited him on Friday nights and on Saturdays, I often passed the Cornells in the parking lot, walking out to their Saabs and Porches and Lexus and Mercedes; it just wasn't that kind of parking lot and so they always parked way out on the far side of the lot to minimize door dings. I parked my Aerostar across the street and hurried to brush past them; sometimes, I stopped to talk to them about Warren. They always had a kind word for me, visiting him this late on Friday. "Your family must miss you," and I would say, "When someone in our community is in trouble like this, I think it is our duty to make sure that they don't feel isolated."

Warren's family could get him out of any fix in a heartbeat, but he didn't want out. He wanted treatment. And he needed it. He wasn't well. They thought he might even be a homosexual, but I didn't know. I suppose with the right medication and the right kind of doctors, people currently can fix just about anything. Nature. Nurture. Chemicals. Genetics. Sexual orientation. It's all so complicated these days. He was such a good Christian.

His voice was hard and loud and hoarse, but he had immaculate timing and such a fervor would overtake him during the singing Sunday morning that we could all hear his abrasive voice. It wasn't difficult to listen to, just spiritually bracing, and made me feel self-conscious about keeping my own volume down.

I pray for Warren and I visit him and talk to him about how he is feeling spiritually and I know he's glad for the company on a weekend when no one else is likely to visit him.

Everyone I tell about visiting Warren doesn't seem to understand, but I understand where they're coming from. They say to me, "If one of his victims was your kid, you'd be pretty angry with this boy." I would be. To think of my child, Martin caught up in all of this.

We had blocked the front broken window pane with a piece of cardboard. It had a Tide logo on it, and I got furious every time I left to go to work because I imagined that an ingenious thief would figure out a way to open the door through that missing panel. Jeff laughed when I told him we needed to get that pane fixed right away. "Lori, a thief that could get through the hole in the window could easily find an easier way into the house. Any place isn't secure against someone determined enough to get in." I didn't understand why he wouldn't protect me.

The bird sat on the fence when I came home, just waiting I'm sure for me to lay my head down for a good snooze. I hurried inside, afraid it would peck out my eyes. Martin came home from soccer. Jeff came home around seven from work. We all sat down at the kitchen table to eat lamb chops and sprouts and I felt as if it was alright, this harried schedule and life I lived. I don't want to say I felt content, because it was too fleeting for that. Contentment is a deep security that you will remain comfortable. We had an alarm system with automatic locks and a direct line to the police station, and I wasn't comfortable.

Already the bird had made several stabs at the house. I listened to the bird cracking into the door. "That's it, I'm going to kill the bird." Martin and Jeff didn't say anything as I pushed back my chair and walked up the stairs. I took the ring of keys hanging in the closet and found the old-fashioned key for the gun case. I slid the cardboard box from under the bed and removed the hard, plastic carrying case.

Martin said, "Mom, that bird is a living thing. If you kill that animal I will never speak to you again."

"What? A threat? You aren't speaking to me now."

"Lori," Jeff said. "Do you really think you are going to kill that bird with a handgun? Nobody has aim like that and certainly not you."

I opened the door and the bird tried to fly through me. I gripped the handgun with one hand and leaned into the door, slamming it shut. The house shook. When I opened the door again, the bird lay on the *Welcome* mat. I grabbed the thing by the back of the neck. It was so light that, for a second, I wondered how it could make enough force to shake our house. I ran into the kitchen.

"Lori!" Jeff said, but I flung the limp bird into one of our freezer bags.

"You're not going to kill it, are you, Mom?" Martin's nasal voice quivered.

"What am I supposed to do?"

Jeff said, "Let's drive it far away and set it free, all right honey?"

"We have to do that," Martin said. "We must."

"You can put the gun down," Jeff said.

I had forgotten that I had it in my hand. My knuckles were white and my pointer finger ached. Jeff gently pulled it out of my hands even though I didn't want to give up that gun. He took that gun and put it back upstairs into its hard, plastic carrying case and put the case into the cardboard box and slid it under the bed.

We drove up into the mountains where it was still a little snowy. But Martin worried the bird wouldn't have any worms or food to eat so high in the mountains, so we drove over the pass and down to Cle Elum. The robin red breast revived at the pass. It started to peep. It spread its beak open and I could see its bright pink tongue, and all of the way down into the insides of the bird and instead of a roar or holler coming out from that bird, a single little note came out. Peep. Martin held it and stroked the short blue and gold feathers on the back of its skull.

In Cle Elum we drove out into the middle of a big field full of yellow flowers and brush. We all got out of the car. It was dusty and warm on the eastside of the mountains. Enormous white clouds escaping from Western Washington flew over the foothills toward the open prairie. The yellow flowers swayed in the wind. Martin lifted the Ziploc bag and the robin red breast struggled out, clawing Martin's hand, and then it flew away. Martin didn't even notice that his hand was all scratched up.

"You'll need to wash that," I told him. But he didn't say anything to me.

We drove home and it was completely dark when we pulled into the driveway. I didn't sleep a wink. I think I was so used to the sound of that animal attacking our house that I couldn't do anything but lie still and wait for it all night.

"Why did you do what you did?" I asked Warren. I finally asked him. I had been wondering and I think trying to ask him in different ways. "You must have known one of those kids would tell."

"I was in love," Warren said. "With those boys. They had everything and I didn't have anything. I am just a guy. I didn't even make it in college. I dropped out as a sophomore and I didn't know what I wanted to do. And these kids had their entire future in front of them; and they knew everything they needed to know about the world and their bodies weren't yet deformed by being fully grown. I mean, before my future came to me, I had it. It was mine. I was an angel at that age."

"A boy is not an angel."

"Yes he is. A boy is perfect. They didn't have a single pimple; their arms were smooth and soft and they didn't sweat and when I kissed them they blushed and smiled and brushed my face with the palm of their hand. I didn't do anything that they didn't want me to do. Yes, I abused my position as a church counselor. I was an older person they respected and trusted. They were relieved to find they had something I wanted so much. If they wanted to give that to me, why would they tell on me? That's what I thought."

"I know what you are saying," I said. "Are you a homosexual?"

"Excuse me, Mrs. Thorton?"

"I didn't think you were one. It had me really worried this whole time. I thought even if your family could save you, that once you were free you would still be in danger of going to Hell."

"That's not why I'm here. I am here because I'm a pedophile. The doctors said they can help me. I can live a normal life one day."

"Sure you can. If they can cure you of liking little boys, then they can cure you of liking big boys."

"I don't think I did this because these children were boys. I didn't want to live with or be with any of these boys. In my mind, I thought everything had stopped for an hour or however long we were together. If I had wanted a relationship with these boys, that would have implied some sort of extended time frame or something. Do you understand that? I just wanted them, instantly, and I wanted that instant to last forever. It wasn't even about sex, I think. It was something else." Warren looked at me for a long time and then shook his head. "Regardless of how my treatment occurs, I don't want to be cured of liking. I want to love someone and I want them to love me."

"You love Jesus. And Jesus loves you."

"Yes, I love Jesus," he said. I looked at Warren in his cell. The linoleum had been scrubbed and buffed to a smooth sheen. Fresh beige paint covered the cement blocks. Warren wasn't looking at me, but examining his hands. They sat in a knot in his lap. He wore a blue shirt and blue slacks. A bad thought crossed my mind then, watching him think whatever he was thinking; I wondered what he thought of when he thought of Jesus. Was Christ erotic to him? If he found little boys erotic because of their purity, then what about Jesus? I, myself, didn't find anything sexual about Him but I did get a thrill on Easter when the church was filled with lilies and the entire congregation filled the nave and Jesus had to notice all of us lined up for His glory.

"I don't like Jesus." Warren didn't untie his hands but his knuckles turned white. "I want to love and like another human being. I can't see myself hanging around my house all day watching TV, and reading books, and listening to CDs with Jesus."

"I understand what you mean."

"Do you?"

"Do I what?

"Do you really understand what I mean? You say that. You come here and talk to me and you always say that. 'I understand what you mean.' Up until five minutes ago, I thought you did understand. I thought when I said something you had empathy and that you naturally responded. Instead I get the sense you come here more the way someone visits and revisits the scene of a bad car wreck or some other disaster area. I don't think you understand anything."

"I call it like it is. We must all live honestly under the eyes of God. Warren, I want to understand."

"You want the wisdom of the pervert?"

"Why did you do what you did?"

"There is a big list of words but they won't explain my actions. I did what I did, I did. But I still want to be cured of what I did. I am here now and this is supposed to be the first step toward being a normal person. Maybe I'll never be normal. One day I'll be like a normal person. That will be enough for me to have the confidence that I have been forgiven."

"I understand," I said. "I really understand what you are saying."

"You do not understand," he said. "Because if you did understand you wouldn't say anything."

"That's crazy. How could you know I understand if I didn't communicate with you? I want to understand why you did what you did. I will keep coming back until we understand each other. I have to know. What did you do to my son?"

"Martin? I never touched that creepy little kid."

"Rape is an act of violence, not love."

"I didn't rape anyone. And you certainly wouldn't see me hanging out with Martin, much less being alone with him."

"You have confessed to fourteen counts of statutory rape; young man, you have raped fourteen anyones."

"You need to leave. Whatever is wrong with your kid isn't my fault."

When I stood up to go, the guard walked slowly down the hallway. The soles of his polished shoes ticked and ticked on the worn green and white linoleum. He smiled at me and slowly scanned the cell. Warren had gone back to just staring at his hands or staring into space, wherever, just waiting until things changed for him, I guess. "Are you on your way out?" the guard asked me.

"Yes, sir," I said. I didn't say goodbye to Warren. He would probably let me see him again. There wasn't anything else for him to do. He'd probably be grateful if I came back. I walked out of the long lines of bars, down the hallway with the narrow safety glass windows, and finally out the front gate. I sat behind the locked steering wheel of my Aerostar, with its steady internal temperature and automatic seatbelt that closed around me and pressed me firmly into place. When I turned the ignition, the steering wheel floated freely in my hands. As I drove home, I wondered why it was necessary for me to drive all of the way out to Monroe to get answers about my own son Martin? I wondered why it was easier for me to answer the guard's questions, walk through three layers of security, to sit in a little cell with someone like Warren who really didn't have anything to tell me about Martin anyway.

That bird, that robin red breast came back that night. He came all of that way, from that field of yellow flowers in Cle Elum to find us. The house shook so much, I thought the chandelier would come loose and shatter on the floor, leaving shards of crystal and bent wire and I would cut my feet in the morning. I woke Martin on the way downstairs. "Your bird is back," I said. He sat up in bed, his eyes glassy, and then finally he slid out of bed. His pajama bottoms bunched around his knees. We stood in the foyer and put our hands on the front door and felt it beat as the robin red breast hurled itself at the battered, brown aluminum door frame. "You aren't going to try and kill it again, are you, Mom?" Martin asked.

"No. If a crazy bird wants to come inside our house so bad, why don't we just let it?" I opened the door and the bird raced inside. The bird perched in the chandelier, sending the whole thing swaying back and forth. The glass chimed and sang. Martin and I stood in front of the open door and watched the bird for a while. I could feel the cold air outside pushing into the house, but I didn't say anything until finally I said, "I'm tired, honey. I'm going back to sleep."

I left the door open for the bird to go when it found whatever it was looking for wasn't here. I went back upstairs and fell asleep even though my front door swung free on its hinges. I fell right asleep even though dollars and dollars worth of heated air flew out into the cool morning and that lunatic bird was somewhere in our house.

# Reverse Order

I BELIEVE IN ROAST BEEF SANDWICHES and Roswell. I do not believe in low-fat mayo or God. Don't make me out for some New Age, Second Coming from Mars freak, it's just as a die-hard atheist I can see through the shit to the truth, like Superman staring directly to the bottom of a Honeybucket. A critical citizen must read between the lines. If the U.S. Government maintains that aliens do not exist, then they must. If the U.S. Government officially denied his existence, I'd believe in God. In the end you can't just trust everything that you touch and feel and know. I myself was abducted and mutilated by aliens the day after my wife, Trudy, flipped out.

Let me tell you about the situation with Trudy. She said, "I'm sitting here, not watching this movie. Dell, do you want to know why?" She held the remote control up with one manicured hand. Her nails, short, crisp and red, sparkled in the TV light as she clicked pause on the video we had been watching together.

"Mom, we're right in the middle," her son Mark said, "turn it back on."

"I would like to make an announcement while I have it

prepared and while the three of us are here together. Can I make my announcement?"

"Can't we wait until the movie is over?"

"One, Dell—we are going to get a divorce. Two, Dell—I am a lesbian and I have always been gay and will remain gay despite any love I may have thought I had for you." She took a breath, a showy drag of air into her lungs. "Three, Dell—my friend, Linda, and I have put down a deposit on an apartment in Wilderness Rim. That's it. We may return to our regularly scheduled programming."

Mark half swallowed and gasped bubbles out of his nostrils. Wiping his face with the back of his hand, he carefully set the can on the kitchen table. He and I sat on the red couch cushions while the video we'd been watching buzzed and clicked on *pause* and then the tape machine turned off and snow poured onto the screen. We had a big TV. It was the only piece of new furniture that Trudy and I had bought together in our fourteen years of marriage. We bought it new right out of the Sears in Bellevue. Everything else was pretty much stuff Trudy and I'd picked up here and there. We'd done all right for ourselves—the sofa may have been a little beat up but I think it had character. It had funky wooden claw legs and Chinese patterns—dragons clawing their way through cliffs and mist. Trudy and I collected all of our furniture together. Sitting in that room, I figured if I just turned the movie back on, whatever she'd just said would fade away like a half-remembered TV commercial. I depressed the *play* and we all sat there not saying anything while the action, adventure, excitement, *ha ha* shot its blue light over us.

Mark asked, "What does that mean?" I shrugged because Trudy's line of argument was news to me. Mark adjusted his pants that were too loose and had slid down to reveal the elastic band of his boxer shorts.

"It means, Honey, that I'm attracted to women. I can only love another woman."

"But you married Dad."

"I was confused. I am sorry."

"You've been confused for that long?"

"Yes. This happens. A person doesn't want to admit what they are. Especially when it has such a big effect on a family. But it doesn't mean I love *you* any less."

"I saw that look," I said.

"I gave you that look," she said.

"But what," Mark said, "if you are confused now? How long have you considered yourself a homo?"

"It's not polite to label me."

"But you said you can only love a woman."

"I love Linda."

"You've been a dyke since before I was born?"

"Linda and I are going to live together."

"I'm not going to live with two homos," Mark said. He stood up from the couch and brushed the kernels of microwave popcorn off his lap. They left small grease stains speckling his pocket and hips. He looked at both of us sitting on the edge of the sofa. I felt like I had been taking a nap in the afternoon, I mean dead asleep when it was pretty light outside, and somebody had just thrown back the curtains. I looked at Mark who hadn't moved for maybe a full second, but it seemed like a long time that he stood there looking both Trudy and me over. Mark melted all of a sudden. He was so much taller than us. His skin seemed pale to me, except when I held my arm to his face I could see that my own skin seemed washed-out. Trudy said that she, herself, was French Indian; but then Trudy said a lot of things about herself. Let me point out that her son isn't my biological son; even so I have raised him with my own two hands with just about as much care as if he was my son. Trudy has never told me who Mark's father was, so I figured it might be somebody I know. I might point out that Mark's biological father was a man, like myself, with whom Trudy had slept more than just the single occasion of Mark's conception. Mark was so much better looking than Trudy and me. Sometimes I thought he was just someone over for a visit to watch TV and eat some free pizza. The muscles in his face just went limp as a cry sloughed out of his mouth. When he melted like this, I realized he was still a kid. I wanted to do the same thing. I just wanted to say, "There's no way I'm married to a homo," and run upstairs with him.

Maybe Trudy and I just weren't meant to be married. She first came to Seattle in the seventies. Trudy was a punk back then. She said she came to the Pacific Northwest because of the floating bridges and because if she went any further west from New York she'd drown herself in the Pacific Ocean. Her orange hair, the safety pin in her nose, the habit of overfilling cups until the coffee drooled over the rim and pooled on the table didn't help her as a waitress at the diner where I was the night cook. I made her take out her pin and the hair dye. She looked sort of matronly and stunned with her welfare glasses and pimples. So instead of scaring the customers, they took pity on Trudy and tipped her all right. But I couldn't do anything about her attitude about refilling a cup of Sanka.

She made a big show out of how tough she was. As the night cook at the time, it was my duty to whip the pain in the ass waitresses into shape by making it hard for them. For their customers, everything was wrong. I cut the sirloin tip roast in half. I cooked the hamburger until the meat turned as rubbery and warped as a toilet plunger. I once placed a long black millipede the bus boy had found in the basement stockroom into a plate of spaghetti. As a result, the waitresses were always sickly sweet to the kitchen crew. Who's going to tip anything on a side of millipede? Unlike everyone else, Trudy didn't get intimidated. She just looked at the insect and said, "Goddamn it. This is a millipede and you ordered a centipede." The long black insect sparkled in the Copper Kitchen's muted light and Trudy kept the bug on the plate and dumped the whole thing, the spaghetti, the blue ringed porcelain plate, and the millipede into the trash.

The first time Trudy met my first wife, she said, "I'm going to fuck your husband." My wife looked Trudy over. Trudy's hair lay congealed under her hair net. Her glasses lay half-crooked on her face. Her gawky arms tucked against her sides as she smoked in the alley behind the diner. My first wife in her dark wool overcoat and perm and fresh lipstick, said, "Honey, you're welcome to try."

Trudy had lived with a woman in Belltown the summer she had first moved to Seattle, displacing the previous lover. One night coming down the stairs from her girlfriend's place, the jilted lover jumped Trudy in the alley. The woman had a pair of brass knuckles and knocked Trudy in the head. When Trudy tells the story, she always talks about how they had tumbled out into the middle of Battery Street, and of course the asphalt is damp because it is Seattle, and of course their scanty garments slick against their skin. They smacked each other. They yanked out hanks of hair. At that point, I always started to get these sexy images of two woman tearing at each other's clothes. I know now that Trudy was probably thinking the same thing because she always threw in a few details, like how she could feel the woman's bra buckle pull apart. The old lover tried to slide her ragged, blue fingernails under Trudy's eyes. Trudy still has scars she tries to hide with concealer. "I screamed and blood started to just pour out of those cuts and I had my hands over my eyes and then the bitch got me in a head lock and I'm thinking that's it, she's going to pop my eyes out like watermelon seeds. Instead she started to wallop me in the skull with a pair of brass knuckles. I didn't know it at the time; I just thought, Jesus Christ this bitch is strong."

Trudy started dating men after that. I figured that her having lived with a woman had just been a part of her punk lifestyle. She used to leave her punk magazines around the diner's break room. The cheap photostats with all kinds of hard to decipher tiny writing looked like someone had hammered out the article on a broken typewriter. It was all so self-consciously brassy.

My first wife was the one who suggested I get together with Trudy. My first wife left me a note in a return envelope to the power company with my name written on the outside in big block letters. I didn't know her handwriting. We'd been married for ten years then and we talked and read books, but I'd never seen her handwriting. So I couldn't figure out what this note was all about, until I read it, naturally. I had to write down the address on a blank envelope for the power bill. That's what I remember from my first wife leaving me. She half-jokingly suggested Trudy when I called her to complain about her being gone. "I'm not coming back. You are just a mean person, Dell. You are such a bastard to people that I didn't think you could be serious. Good heavens, I even thought it was cute sometimes when you would throw a tantrum at the kitchen and rip off your chef hat and throw some poor waitress's food into the dumpster. I thought it was a means to an end, but now I see it's just meanness. Why don't you call Trudy? She always had a thing for you." My first wife hung up on me. I stood in the pay phone booth holding the heavy cold phone receiver to my ear. I flopped open the ratty White Pages and called Trudy.

I married Trudy in a blaze of divorce settlement cash. I said, *yes, I'd marry you* on the Snoqualmie Railroad train that ran on the last of the Milwaukee-Seattle line just above the Snoqualmie Falls. The preacher wore mutton chops and a monocle. It was a western costume wedding. I bought Trudy five hundred dollars of lace and a tiara with real pearls and a black satin choker. I wore cowboy boots, a silver sheriff star, and a black tux for a man slightly taller than myself.

I had insisted I knew my size and the young clerk in his own loosely fitting tuxedo and thin mustache assured me I that must be fitted. "This won't fit like a suit," he had said. I'm not a man to wear a tie much less a suit. But Trudy had wheedled me into financing a dress-up wedding. "I know my size," I had said. "After all, I am my size." But I hadn't known my size. I had to roll up the cuffs.

I was nervous and happy and on cocaine. A little powder helped me celebrate. It threw the whole thing into an echo chamber for me to relish each reverberating second. I certainly needed that ecstatic moment to last as long as possible.

That was probably the last time I had cause for celebration in my fourteen years married to Trudy. I did have a life with her; most things worked out all right. She lived in my house for fourteen years with her son Mark growing up as my own son. I worked four days a week for many years so that I could spend more time in the mountains and be a father to that boy. Trudy worked fifty odd hours for the phone company in a big mirror covered building in Bellevue. She handled corporate accounts all day and came home to her Molson Ice. I kept the beer cold and in stock. Everything seemed fine. Like most things, I guess, a whole lot was going on below the surface that in hindsight I know was keeping me awake at night. But at the time, while I lay in bed sweating and clenching the pillow in a full-nelson, I thought that I'd drunk too much coffee or took a little too many heart-shaped pills Thursday night, that it was something I'd done or taken that was keeping me awake at night.

I woke early the morning after Trudy's announcement with a dreadful conviction that I had to go into the mountains.

Something was out there; something hovered in the grayish clouds of mist; something hung over the sharp gray cliffs of the Cascade Mountains; something wanted me to go out there. A light drizzle fell onto the lawn. Heavy gray clouds billowed down close to the tops of the old fir trees growing behind the house. We lived in the last place before the tracts of Weyerhaeuser second-growth.

I called the secretary's voice mail and told her I couldn't come in today. I worked at a sewage treatment plant in Kirkland where I had worked since I quit my job as a cook. I didn't get promoted often, but I left my work at work. I didn't get calls from the office. I said, "I'm sick today. I won't be in. My wife left me." I mean why lie? She'd tell everyone and I'd have a sympathy card and some treats and I wouldn't have to say anything to their faces about what had happened.

When Trudy made her confession, I must admit that I knew something was going on. For awhile I thought the hours she worked at her office were just the novelty of her recent promotion; working a job she was good at was a new thing. The official recognition they gave her came along with a lot of baggage. She received calls from work after her promotion. Sometimes I answered and there would be Linda at the other end, or sometimes the loud voice of her boss Gary. Those two were always a little too friendly, raising their voice to this beer-hall, fake-friend bark; "How ya doing Dell? Good. Can you put Trudy on the line?" Trudy's job followed her everywhere. When we had gone hiking last summer, she had brought her spreadsheets printed and stapled into a booklet. I had sat on the shore of a lake on one of the scratchy gray stones with my feet in the water and Trudy had sat under the blue pine trees and, for all she was worth talking to, she had left me a long time ago; I needed a cell phone just to talk to her, even though it was just her and me up there in the mountains. I figured there was no use lying about it. My wife had already passed on.

I drank my coffee while I waited for Trudy to wake up. She came downstairs finally in nylons and her blue pin-striped skirt and her red plastic briefcase that I always thought looked like a really big lunch box. "Don't you think we should talk about this?" I asked.

"It would just make you frustrated or mad or both. You think you can talk your way out of my being the way I am?"

"What are you Popeye the Sailorman now? I yam what I yam."

"Let me talk you out of being an asshole. Tried it. Didn't work. There isn't anything to be done. It doesn't matter if you were genetically predisposed to be an asshole or just decided to be an asshole."

"If you are mad at me, then I apologize. I am sorry for whatever I did. But if you are just mad at me because I'm a man, that's ludicrous. I wish I could believe that you are gay, Trudy. So you're having sex with women. That doesn't mean you have to move into your own apartment to have unchecked sex with a woman. That's just sex. I could have sex with a man. Hell, I could have sex with a donkey. But that doesn't mean I'm gay. For that matter, it doesn't mean I'm a donkey. Sex, to me, seems to be what you are equating with your identity. You are committing to being gay or being straight as if it's like hair color and the fact that you've been married to a man was merely like fourteen years of passing for a blonde. You married me knowing I was a man. I assume you married me; you didn't marry a sexual orientation."

"Well, I don't know. You go out into the mountains, Dell, and formulate your come-back plan. Be back home by sunset. I'm not going to wait around for you to make an even bigger ass out of yourself." She climbed into her black Toyota and left the same as if it were just any other morning.

Before I could formulate a come-back plan, I was abducted by aliens. I lost six hours. Maybe it was a force of nature, but I'm pretty sure it was a technology not of this earth. Something happened where I lost some time. Six hours and some change. Six hours is not like a wallet; it can't fall out of my pocket.

Here's how it happened. I had one of my pukers. Sometimes I hike to the point of exhaustion and then I keep hiking until I'm lying on the side of the trail with the dry heaves. It was dusk when I finally ran down the rutted trail from the mountain into the tall fir trees that grow by the river. In the twilight, my white clothes always seem to glow when I finally get out into the open air in the road. Everything else loses its color in comparison. My hands, for instance, looked the same as the dirt.

At nightfall, the birds start to sing loud. At dusk, it is just the wild last minute party before the sun finally slips over the ridge and the darkness creeps up the valley floor.

So in this noisy dusk, half drowsy from my hike, anticipating the weightless comfort of man-made, cushioned seats, I climbed into my truck. I remembered looking at the time on my wristwatch to check how late I would be because I had told Trudy I'd be home by dark which was 7:30 and my watch said it was 7:10. I had gone into the mountains to clear my head, but I still wasn't sure how I would deal with her. I did know I needed to get home before she left, I didn't want to screw up my last chance.

I judge time in the mountains by the light. Peaks and valleys and basins and gorges throw off the light. A peak stands out into the daylight like an island holding onto dusk while the blackness of full nighttime creeps up the lower slopes. I stood in the cleft of a valley, so I figured everything was all right when I started my car. I started to drive down the valley toward the main Weyerhaeuser gate and then the highway. Next thing I knew, it had become dark. I kept driving and I drove over the

Wagonner Bridge. The complete darkness didn't really register at first. I kept driving and I looked up and noticed, then, the sharp black outline of the fir trees against a sky full of stars. I thought it had become really dark, really fast. I checked my watch. It was 1:10, now, 1:10 in the morning.

The truck bumped over the potholes. I immediately stopped the rattling engine. I could hear the moan of the river and the rustle of the fir boughs. The gauge read half full just like it did when I had started the truck. I looked up at the stars and they were just a wash of trillions of little specks, more like discoloration and pitted marks in the dome of the sky than little suns glittering light through the trillion miles of space. There are things that happen in the universe beyond my control or understanding that have a bigger effect on my life than any single act I have planned. Six hours had evaporated.

I must have been in the car a long time because my thighs felt chaffed and sticky in my jeans. My shirt also felt tight in strange places. My heart felt closed off in a wad of fat, which is a strange feeling after coming down from the mountains. Usually I feel sort of loose and light headed and hungry. But I felt like my skin was french toast right before I toss it onto the frying pan and it's dripping butter and whipped eggs. My plaid cotton shirt lay plastered to my sticky skin. I wanted to peel off my clothes. I've heard that sometimes people going through unbearable stress just shut down and go to sleep. I had plenty to worry about.

I pulled the truck under a stand of cedar trees. A crick ran way down in a gully hidden behind the trees and bushes and down past the deadfalls. Before I got out of the truck, I stared at the woods. There wasn't anything out there in the reddish trunks of the cedar trees or the leafy bracken fern. I noticed, then, in the light of the truck that my hands didn't have any hair. My arms were smooth and hairless. I even imagined that my fingers seemed a little shorter than they had before I had fallen asleep, passed out, just shut down or whatever had happened.

I could've been suffering, too, from the hike. I usually dropped weight out there, which didn't account for how bloated I felt. I hiked so vigorously, I once lost ten pounds in one day. It was as if I melted under the sun on the steep hillsides. But my hands seemed so much smaller. I pulled my gloves out from under the front seat. They were loose and stained with motor oil, but in the past they had fit. Now they floated around my hands. It dawned on me that I had been shaved. Those aliens had performed experiments on me.

This isn't an easy thing to realize. I felt suddenly antiseptic, like I had passed out at the dentist's office and he'd continued to clean my teeth. I had my wisdom teeth out, a while ago. I stared up into the dentist's overheard light and then he cupped the mask to my face and the room turned blurry as he scraped my teeth and I woke some time later, heavy and sweating on the chair. The first thing I smelled was the metallic odor of the equipment sterilizer. I felt this aching absence of my wisdom teeth. I probed with my tongue and felt loose flaps of skin and the holes right into my jaw bone.

I locked the door to the truck then, but left the cab light on to examine everything on myself to see if I could find something. I squirmed in the bucket seat, behind the steering wheel and realized that if the aliens were looking, they could see me like I was in a shop window. I even had props, the stacks of daily newspaper in the back, the brown McDonald's breakfast bags, and me. Even if my truck was locked and driving, that hadn't stopped the aliens from abducting me and stealing six hours and all of my hair.

Examining my face in the rear view mirror, I saw that not only did I not have a beard anymore, but I didn't even have whiskers or hair follicles. I still had the hair on my head. I still had eyebrows. I wiggled them. They looked like they had been plucked.

I jumped out of the truck onto the muddy side of the road, listening to the toads in the damp crick gully croak and the river groan way down in the valley. I stood out of the truck on the side of the road under the dark trees. The truck looked the same as it always did on the road. Fingers of hardened mud spread out from the chrome edges of the wheel wells. The dent just behind the passenger side door still went in. I felt my skin under my T-shirt. It was cold outside and I felt the air slip under my shirt as I ran my hands over my warm stomach and rib cage, touching the soft flesh on my back but everything felt whole. I didn't feel any strange marks or pimples or dimples, no physical signs of alien abduction. It was like I had been put on pause. Maybe I was just tired and fell asleep before I started the car and dreamed I had started driving toward the highway. I was afraid to strip—what would I find under my soaked shirt? Strange tattoos marking out the choice pieces of my flesh for alien gourmets? A weasel had clawed into my chicken coop one night and removed a hunk of flesh from the soft back of one of the prime gray and white speckled egg laying hens—as neatly as if the chunk of meat was a puzzle piece. Would I have all of my pieces, or would I find a neat incision where my delicious appendix had been?

Undoing the buttons to the shirt, I was surprised by the fleshly, doughy hang to my chest. I had put on weight with all of the hidden stress of Trudy running around and I've always been a man with over abundant pectoral muscles. Lately, I had even remarked to Trudy that I was getting pretty nice jugs. I had once looked into getting a breast reduction with a plastic surgeon but my insurance wouldn't cover any of the treatment and Trudy talked me out of it. What a surprise, now, her not talking me out of tit removal. She must have relished the hang of my chest as I drilled her, back when she allowed me drilling rights. With my skin shaved for whatever alien probe I had undergone, I really looked like a woman now. Maybe I could trick Trudy?

I shook now with my cold, damp skin exposed in the forest. A cool wind came down the valley. I pulled my pants down past my hips. I felt bloated. I had developed quite large love handles. Oddly, I had lost a lot of weight around my waist. A regular hourglass figure.

I slid my pants over my damp skin, turning my jeans inside out. Something ticked in the woods. I stood there caught with my pants bunched around my boots, staring into the forest. I didn't see anything out there. I fell against the side of the truck. Looking in the mirror, I saw how full my lips became when I was terrified. Even though I had been shaved smooth, the aliens had generously left me a nice muff of pubic hair. I couldn't find my penis, which I wouldn't miss. I don't think I was that frightened. I am not a notably well-endowed man, but my thing is a noticeable hang of stuff, what with a scrotum, penis head, and so on. Instead, I found a neat incision. Is this what these bastards were after? Is this what the aliens are harvesting from remote mountain regions?

I searched the cab of the truck. I pulled out the pockets of my jeans. I looked through my backpack. I couldn't find it. I only found an unopened can of beer under the seat. I popped it and drank the frothy warm fluid straight down and put on a pair of dry shorts and a dry T-shirt. I wasn't bleeding from the cut. It didn't feel sore. I couldn't think of anything except its absence. The joints of my arms felt like the dowels had jolted loose. This was far worse than having my wisdom teeth out.

Where there had been a slight and not unpleasant ache between my legs when I sat in the chair, there was nothing now, just the squash of my bloated thighs.

I drove home keeping one eye on the dark forest and one eye on the road, and constantly staring up into the starry sky not sure what I'd do if I saw those bastards. I'd either hide for fear of what they'd do to me next or I'd be angry enough to demand they set me right or kill me outright.

I also blamed myself. I had known that if I went into the mountains today, of all days, something was bound to happen, considered how distraught I was. I'd had a premonition. But I don't listen to those kinds of things and now I was an alien mutilated man with a lesbian for a wife.

The dining room light shone out through the dark kitchen when I came home. Trudy sat at the dining room table. I had caught her. She snuffed out her cigarette. "Where have you been?" She poured her mug of coffee down the sink. She always used the mug with fish painted on the blue surface. It had a broken handle and I had meant to throw it out, but she liked to drink coffee out of it so I didn't throw it out. The broken handle gouged the palm of my hand when I drank from it and the ceramic got way too hot, so I had to wait it out. Trudy sloshed her coffee into the sink. "Are you going to say something?" Under her voice I could hear everything else. She could start shouting at any second. I still didn't know if I had irrevocably screwed it up, yet.

"I shouldn't have waited for you," she said.

Didn't she notice that I didn't have a beard anymore? "Excuse me," I said. I turned on the bathroom light and looked into the mirror. I was a woman. I realized then, the aliens had made me a woman. "I am a woman!" I shrieked because the woman who stood in the bathroom on the other edge of the mirror wasn't like anyone I would even look at twice. I looked into the mirror and saw a gawky, donkey of a woman, a PTA mother, a suburban insurance-hut secretary suffering from bronchitis. I couldn't believe I made such a poor female specimen.

Trudy has said she liked to have sex with women. Therefore, that made her a homosexual. When I asked her why she was leaving me for Linda, she had said, "It isn't your fault if that is what you think. You're male; she's female." To me sex with someone was a complex ledger book of desire. I think of it as a cracked leather ledger written with an old fountain pen in spidery handwriting with a pale green rule on cream paper and maybe the rings of a coffee cup on a few of the pages from late night fretting over the numbers. My ledger book would have to have lots of fretting. All of this was supply and demand, that is *need*. I do not discount entirely the simplistic arithmetic of desire. Trudy wanted a woman.

"I am a woman," I said. "Will you love me?"

She looked at me and then she shook her head. "I'm sorry, honey, women do not have this." She grabbed my crotch and somehow re-attached my lost penis. As if she had thrown the throttle, my chest hair and back air and forearm hair poured out. There was now a man standing on the rim of the bath tub. I examined my bristles of back hair running along the fat funnel of my spine and the bundle of fat bunched around my belly button and the loose slippery dangle of my penis and testicles. I was detestably male. Linda was not these things. She was female. You may need a glass of water and a mug of water just won't do. I do not discount the power of mathematical logic. A mug doesn't equal a glass of water and a man doesn't equal a woman. But it is still water, gaddamn it. I still needed Trudy to be in this house. I didn't ask much. Just someone to push around now and then.

"I am married to you," I said. "I want to be married to you."

Trudy had one of my old suitcases packed, an aquamarine handbag, faded almost white with a sticker on it that was sun-bleached almost white. It was my suitcase and she was packing her things into it and would take it to her house and I would never see it again. My mother bought me the suitcase when we went to stay with my great aunt in Iowa the summer I was fifteen. My father had moved out of the house and she moved me to her great aunt's house. I put the sticker on it; Washington the Evergreen State and I stored my *Little Lulu* comic books and *Hardy Boy's* books in the suitcase on the train ride to Iowa. The sticker wasn't green anymore; it was just the fuzzy paper silhouette of a tree. I didn't say anything to Trudy because I liked it that she was putting all of things into something of mine that I had owned years before I had even heard of her.

"I'm leaving," she said. She closed the sliding glass door behind her. I was left in the house with Mark sleeping upstairs, but I was alone. I watched her car drive back down the driveway, the headlights shining through the misty rain. The lights receded into the darkness. It was just the actual rain falling trough the actual boughs of the trees and this was my actual house and even if I had been abducted by aliens and they had returned me to a reverse planet to watch me squirm, Trudy was still gone.

# Mother's Milk

Trips to Victoria amused Ed because his wife was named Victoria. She claimed her name was written as Vicky on birth certificate. "I was christened Victoria, but my real name is Vicky. I despise any person who tries to call me Victoria." She had been going by Victoria for as long as Ed had known her. When her mother called for her Sunday afternoon chat, she always asked, "Can I speak to Victoria?" This name adjustment was a new thing. Not as new as Victoria's recent delivery of Alex, Ed's son, six months ago, but her retroactive name change coincided neatly with her pregnancy, and Victoria's transformation from a bony, pretty young woman into an excessively beautiful, abundantly ample mother, and the complete and utter cessation of all things conjugal between her and her husband.

Already at twenty-two Ed had gray hairs in his temple and beard. He drove a truck for the city of Tacoma daily newspaper. One of the reporters he knew asked him to come to a party, but when Ed showed up, no one said anything to him. Some of the older reporters played cards in the back bedroom at a card table and everyone else drank beer from plastic cups and stood in dense clumps with their backsides forming a faceless, impenetrable wall. *The Tacoma News Tribune*, to be precise, was a third-rate daily paper in a region infamous for its second-rate daily newspapers. Victoria worked there as a fact checker, a job she had found after working at the paper as a work-study student for her first and only quarter of college. She was slim, brown, and had long kinky hair. She wore a silver barrette fashioned like a peacock and a floor length floral dress featuring magnolia leaves on a black background. "I'm too old to pick up a fool," she said to Ed. "Are you a fool?" Ed didn't answer because he wasn't sure what she wanted to hear, which was exactly what she wanted to hear.

His wife had thick teeth with square caps. When she spoke, her very red tongue with so-red-they're-almost-purple taste buds flashed against the caps of her teeth. He saw her as she was at that party, eyes heavy with a beer too many and talking in a too loud voice. Ed always stood near her as if he were inside a room with the four walls of her voice. He thought, too, of something she said after they'd left the party. "It must be your cologne, Ed," she'd said, "because what we're dealing with here is something chemical. I can't explain it."

"Thank you anyway," he'd said.

There are fat women who aren't big women (fat men, too), and there are skinny women who are big women. Victoria was a big woman before she was overweight. Overweight, she was enormous. Her weight manifested itself in rolls around her stomach, a bunching of flesh at the tops of her arms and legs, although she moved without any sign of stress. She didn't sweat or wobble. When she climbed stairs, she needed only to pause to catch her breath at the very top, a brief draw of breath.

Her long neck provided a good frame for her fleshy head.

Her short hair, still black but thick with tiny shreds of silver, caught the daylight in azure arcs. Her red or brown skin was, on closer inspection, slightly translucent, so that the observer became aware of several layers of color, rust and then mole specks floating in a brown field.

When she spoke, her voice had a clear resounding timbre, and she spoke constantly or laughed or shushed and filled the air in a twenty foot radius. She walked through the house wearing one of Ed's old oxfords with Alex sprawled out on the shelf of flesh below her breasts. When Alex began to fuss, she unbuttoned the shirt and attached his head to her nipple. Now that she had finally grown into the name Victoria, she said, "Oh no. My name is Vicky. It's always been Vicky. What are you talking about, Victoria? Who's that? Do I look like a Victoria?" when actually, she did.

Ed's parents ran a silent house in Wallingford, Seattle. Radios, TVs, phonograph players had been banned from their living space. Drink, tobacco, Kool-aid, any foodstuff that didn't directly contribute to a healthful diet had been banned. They had exiled clutter. No magazines or framed photographs. The sole bookcase had a lead glass front and held the 1962 edition of the *Encyclopedia Britannica* and a green calf-bound set of Dickens. Every Sunday, Ed's family woke and drove to the Methodist Church Ed and his father cleaned on Wednesday nights. Ed hardly remembered the services now, but he clearly remembered the smell of Simple Green (his father's favorite cleaning solvent) in a tin bucket. Ed twisted the handle of the mop while gripping the shoestring thick fibers. The smell of Simple Green lingered in the hallways, even on Sunday. They always began in the meeting hall in the basement, his father sweeping first with the flat broom to pull down cobwebs from the ceiling, knocking down spiders and little flecks of the ceiling texture, and then using a dust mop to make a neat pile. He leaned down to whisk it into a copper dustpan. As soon as he'd worked halfway across the room, Ed began to mop. He could hear his father whistling in the hallway ahead of him. "April in Paris" or "Ain't Misbehaving" came out half-remembered and then echoed on the cement walls. After they had cleaned the main hall and packed everything into the van, they sat on the steps and Ed's father let Ed smoke a single cigarette. The first time this happened, he was unsure what he was supposed to do. He wondered if this was some kind of test his father was putting him through. "Go ahead and smoke it."

"Mom says you shouldn't."

"Pah," Ed's father said.

His father leaned over and lit the cigarette, and Ed let half of it burn before he took a tentative pull at the end. The taste of it, a heavy and sweet burn, filled his mouth. He coughed. His eyes began to water, but he didn't throw it away because his father had given it to him. They sat on the steps and he tried not to cough. His father smiled. "Next time, you won't cough so much. Or waste so much."

Gradually as Ed began to smoke the whole thing, he came to believe that if a person did a little of the work that they didn't want to do, that gave them a little room to do the things they wanted to do. He wasn't sure, if given the choice, he'd have chosen a cigarette. But after a summer, he began looking forward to hearing his father whistle old songs and then sitting down to smoke with him on the dark church steps at eleven o'clock at night.

On the trip to Victoria, Ed stood with his wife in line with their passports out. She showed him her name on her passport. "Vicky," she said. She looked around her for a second and then said, "Before we get on the boat, call Marilyn and see how my baby is doing."

"The baby is fine. Marilyn has kids. They're all alive."

"Her daughter had a cast at twenty-five months. That's young to have something serious enough for you to break bones. Very young. Babies have soft bones. A mother can only break a baby's bones by watching the baby fall down a flight of stairs or backing her truck over them. It takes some work to break a baby."

"Marilyn doesn't drive a truck," Ed said. "Nothing's going to happen."

"Why did you say that? Do you think something's happened? You are psychic. You don't know it but you are. You say things, and they come to pass."

"I have good follow-through."

"You can't refuse it. It's a gift. Who doubts a skeptical prophet?"

"I've turned down gifts before."

"Can you find a phone?"

"We're almost through the line."

They handed their passports to the boarding clerk.

"Occupation?"

"Welder," Ed said.

"Mother," Victoria said.

When they were on the other side, Victoria called home. "Marilyn what's happened? Ed's had a vision. Is Alex all right? Broken leg? Ed saw Alex with a cast on. Can you wake him up to make sure he is still, you know, alive? I don't want you to just make sure he's breathing. He could be brain-damaged and in a coma and still drawing breath. If you could make sure his pupils dilate—sorry. No, we're not on the ferry yet. We're about to board now, which is why I called. We can come home right now if you think it's too much. Yes. Call as soon as it happens." Victoria flung her phone back into her purse. "I don't think we should have left him with her."

"Marilyn is the best mother there is. No one is more qualified to look after our son."

"His own mother might be a sliver more qualified."

"I didn't say—"

"We should go back. Any enjoyment for myself has been damned to hell. It's pointless."

"Don't do this now," Ed said. "We have to learn to do things, just you and me. Alex is fine. He's in good hands. Not as good as yours, certainly, but he's safe. We really need some time alone."

"I couldn't even tell if he was breathing. Use your vision to see if he's breathing."

"He's breathing."

"How many beats a minute does his heart beat?"

"90."

"112, sleeping. You shouldn't need second sight to know that. What's my blood?"

"You're East Indian Carob Indian, Chinese, Spanish, Irish—"

"—my blood *type*," Victoria said.

"O negative?"

"AB. That's not a small detail."

"What's my blood type?"

"O negative."

"So, what does that tell you? You know my blood type. That doesn't tell you anything about me. Now I know your blood type. Do I know anything about you because you're AB?"

"I need to go home to check if he's breathing."

Ed and Victoria stood now under the gangplank. They smelled the brine and kelp and the sun-heated, creosote-soaked docks. Swells came across the Sound. Sail boats congregated in a still patch in the middle of the strait. A thick, rusted cargo ship slowly inched along toward Harbor Island, and the caps of the Olympic Mountains were white. The sky pushed down on them, a burnished, scratched cyan. They were outside and would soon be in another country than their child. Ed had plans for the weekend, and he didn't want to go back into their house with Alex crying every half-hour attached to Victoria's chest like a fifteen pound leech with opposable thumbs. "We have to go," Ed said.

"Our baby's death is on your hands if you make me go on this trip."

"Our baby isn't going to die."

"Say it."

"Our baby's death is on my hands."

"You love Alex don't you?"

Victoria asked him this every now and then always quickly, and he wondered if she was looking to catch him off guard. They made their way up the gangplank and into the throbbing passenger deck and found two seats. The boat smelled like rust and fresh paint. People read papers and drank coffee and talked in soft voices. The sun, which had been cool outside, was hot under the windows.

"Can I get you anything?" she asked after the ship pulled away from the dock and was on its way. "Would you like a cup of coffee and a cookie? A brownie?"

"A cup of coffee sounds great. Where's the galley?"

"You stay right here," she said. "I'll get it."

He watched her cross the deck. He wondered if she had thought of some way of jumping ship. Fetching things belonged to his roster of vital activities. While he waited, Ed picked up a loose sheet of the daily paper and read. Every now and again, he would stand up and find himself rocking back and forth, the motion he used with Alex to soothe him, but he stood there with his paper in his hands rocking back and forth and he wasn't really aware of it until he stood up and started rocking as Victoria came back with two coffees and two brownies.

"What's wrong?" she asked him.

He didn't want to say, because she'd start in again on Alex. "Thanks." He had trouble unwrapping the cling-wrapped brownie. Victoria took it out of his hands and unwrapped it for him, leaving the cling wrap around the brownie in a loose band. She handed it back to him, placing the band into his fingers. "There you go," she said.

He ate his brownie and drank his coffee and resisted the urge to stand and rock. They both stared out at the slowly moving shore, the choppy waves. He could see their reflection in the window, the shadow of their heads and the light reflected from their eyes.

Victoria leaned in with a paper napkin she had somehow wetted and wiped Ed vigorously on the corners of his mouth. It stung. He stood up hurriedly and started rocking side to side. "Ouch," he said.

"What are you doing?"

"I could ask the same thing."

He sat back down and finished his coffee. Victoria opened her bag and took out the book she'd been reading before Alex had been born, *A Regular Guy*, the book she'd taken to the hospital to read while she was in labor. She thought she'd be there for a while and had made a lot of plans to distract herself while she was getting ready to give birth. Instead she went from mild discomfort to three days of wheezing and panting and squeezing Ed's hand. She didn't get a lot of reading done.

She didn't get a lot of reading done after the baby was born either or much of anything else.

Ed thought that maybe once they were in Victoria, they could get a room and get back to the business that had gotten them into the situation in the first place. He didn't know how to bring it up with Victoria and was hoping the situation would present itself. He'd already made arrangement with Marilyn in case they stayed over. He said, "We might not make it back tonight if you know what I mean. We might be staying overnight, so if you'd be willing to stay overnight, we can stay overnight if you know what I mean."

"Please," Marilyn had said. "I know what you mean and I don't need to know anymore."

After Alex, Ed waited six weeks to bring *it* up. He came home from work and cleaned the house. He worked hard at work. He kept the house as clean as he could. He did a lot of things he really didn't want to do, because he thought at some point this would entitle him to some of the things he wanted to do. Victoria sat on the couch with the baby and watched him. "Would you like something to eat?" he asked.

"I ain't cooking," she said.

"I'll make it."

"What were you thinking of making?"

"An omelet?"

He took out a candle from the box of votives next to the fine silverware drawer. He lit the candle and then made the omelet. He went out to his truck and came back in with the bottle of wine. She was already half-way through her omelet. Alex clung to her chest, his little head under her shirt.

"Would you like some wine?" he asked.

"I'm breast-feeding."

"They said you could have a glass of wine."

"They did say that," she said. He filled her glass up. He poured wine up to the rim.

"That's too much."

"You don't have to drink it all."

But she drank it all. And when Alex finally fell asleep, she peeled him off her body and lay him down in their bed.

Everything about Victoria was different. She weighed less than she had when she was pregnant, but still she was much larger than she had been before she was pregnant. She smelled strongly of milk, and milk that had begun to cheese. Her breasts, too, were round and heavy and chapped. Although her period hadn't started yet, she could begin ovulation and they didn't want another baby so soon, or maybe not even another baby at all. They didn't want to get any living sperm into her. She applied a vaginal suppository and lubed up with spermicide. He wore a thick condom that caught on the first try in his pubic hair and then as he adjusted it, he got clear fluid, pre-ejaculate, Victoria called it, on the tip and so he had to open another one and this time carefully held his pubic hair down and rolled it quickly into place before he lost his erection in the smell of breast milk and various lethal ointments and the sound of Alex snoring on the other side of the bed. "Do you think," Ed asked. "Don't you think it might be a good idea if—"

"He's asleep," Victoria said. "If you want to fuck me, you better hop on up."

As soon as he'd hopped on up and wiggled the head of his penis into her, he felt something odd, a flap of skin that hadn't been there before, a tightness, and then Victoria grunted and said, "that doesn't feel right. I don't think the doctor sewed me up right."

"Am I hurting you?" He withdrew and that was it, he lost everything, his erection, the condom, and his idea that they could return to their former days of inarticulate love making. Everything now had a name and a procedure and was completely associated with the baby they just had and the babies they didn't want to have.

It seemed like they had really arrived someplace when they drew into the Port of Victoria. Gigantic stones and ancient, imperial cement embankments lined the shore. There were pastel condos being constructed up on the hills overlooking the harbor and Ed didn't even mind that. Victoria was the place to be. He wouldn't want to live in one of those condos. He preferred houses with four walls that belonged to him. He had made reservations for afternoon tea at the hotel.

They disembarked from the ship and passed through customs and wandered through the city. At a bookstore, they both bought books. To Ed, this promised in Victoria a kind of hope that she would have enough time to finish the book. If she had time to read, then she had time for a lot of things. They bought a bag of British candy at a candy store and Victoria walked along unrolling the bag to sort through the candy and then rolling the bag back up. She had hard, round aniseed balls, sugary cola cubes, and soft milk bottles. They sat on a bench overlooking the bay. Then he noticed wet spots on Vicki's chest. "You spilled something on yourself, honey."

She touched her breast as she looked down and then smelled the tips of her fingers. "Milk," she said. "It's time to feed Alex."

"I'll be right back," she said and returned sometime later and Ed couldn't see any sign that she'd been leaking.

At the Empress Hotel, she smiled at the sign that said, "You will be refused service if you are wearing jeans."

"Are you wearing jeans?" she asked Ed.

"You can see I'm not," he said.

"But chinos. Those are pretty informal. I don't know if they'll let you in here."

"They'll let me eat here," he said. "Money is good anywhere."

They were seated in the rattan chairs in the middle of the dining room set for afternoon tea. The waiter put down a tea pot wrapped in a tea cozy and left. "They really know how to do things in style in England," she said.

"This is Canada," Ed said.

"It used to be England," she said. "Hence the name. You know what they say about New Zealand?"

They sat there and he waited for her to tell him. He didn't know what they said about New Zealand. Finally he said, "Well, what do they say about New Zealand?"

"More British than the British," she said. "That's what they say about New Zealand."

"Do they?"

"And that isn't England, either."

"I haven't heard that," he said.

"You haven't heard that?"

"I travel in different circles than you, I guess," Ed said. He meant this, but he smiled, because she always used the word "circles" and he thought people either knew or didn't know each other. Victoria had been born in Trinidad and raised, she said, in an English boarding school. She didn't speak with a British accent, though, and recently even her Trinidadian accent had begun to fade.

The waiter brought a heavy china plate heaped with berries, jars of jam and marmalade, scones, crumpets, preserves, pastries, tarts, and sandwiches. The waiter leaned forward and deposited the plate in the middle of the table. "What else can I get you?" he asked. He said you as "choo."

Ed said, "I'd like some coffee."

When he left, Victoria looked after him. "Not a lot of polish on that guy. You'd think at a place like this they'd send them out for etiquette training or something. It is probably rude to order coffee."

"They have coffee in England," Ed said.

He noticed that wet spots had returned to her breasts. Ed looked around at the people drinking their tea. "You're leaking again," he whispered. "Is there something I can do?"

"I don't know what you should do, but I know what I should do, only Alex is in America and I'm here."

"This is America," Ed said.

She stood up and looked around her at the other tables. They were busy eating and didn't notice her. She regally walked across the lobby room and went to the restroom. While she was gone, the waiter returned with the coffee—a cup of hot water and a pack of instant coffee, sugar, and non-dairy creamer. The waiter didn't say anything but continued on his way.

When Victoria returned from the bathroom, she had two stains on the front of her dress and he could see a piece of toilet paper sticking out of her cleavage. "They brought your damn coffee," she said.

They ate the tea until they were full but it didn't fill Ed up the way a proper meal would fill him up. Victoria held the shopping bag to her chest as they left. They walked down the steps and into the rose garden feeling the weight in their stomachs. They walked on the crushed gravel trail. Ed enjoyed the solid crush of the rocks under his feet. They stopped under an arbor. Victoria looked up through the crossing vines and full heavy roses that had started to turn at the edges of the petals. The smell under the arbor was thick and sweet, rotting vegetation, a fermented pleasant odor. Vicki's hair was jet black and kinked in tight undulations over her scalp and ended just over her brown neck.

Ed leaned forward and brushed his lips on her neck waiting for her to turn around and kiss him. He could smell an odd, sour smell up close to her. It was her breast milk.

But she took a step away and looked at him with a puzzled expression and grabbed her breasts and dropped the bag onto the walkway.

"Maybe we should get that room?" he asked. Even though he had not officially brought up his plan to Victoria, he thought if he just pretended that they'd talked about it, that they'd made plans, it would happen.

"They are about to burst. Ed, they really hurt."

Ed didn't say anything. He didn't quite understand what she was talking about.

"My breasts hurt. We have to go home, honey."

"How do other women handle it?" he asked. "They must do something."

"I don't know," Victoria said. "But I can't do anything."

They walked back to the ship and waited and she stared over the harbor, breathing slowly in and out. "They are going to burst."

"Don't say that."

"It's true. I'm going full tilt. My breasts will rupture."

"That can't happen."

"They are going to split."

"Has that ever happened to anyone? To anyone in history?"

"I don't know if it has happened. Maybe this is the first time. Who knows? But, I'm telling you it will happen."

"What normally happens?"

"Normally Alex drinks it. Maybe Marilyn can meet us at the dock?" She became quiet. They walked up the queue and found seats looking out into the harbor. When the engines started, Victoria grabbed him. "Come on." She took him into the women's bathroom.

"I'm not going in there," he said as she took him in.

She tore off her shirt and pulled her bra down, exposing a boob. A film of milk covered her breast. "Drink it down," she said.

"What if someone comes in?"

"No one will come—" and the door opened and then closed.

Ed *had* been curious. He wasn't a squeamish man about bodily fluid. He did what he needed to do. But that was one thing and this seemed more utilitarian, like lancing a boil with his teeth or cleaning her ears with the tips of his fingers.

"I *have* to get the milk out of my boobs, Ed," she said.

He lowered himself down to his knees, and she held her breast up to him like a loose water balloon. A thick drop rolled out of the thin round lip of the nipple. The nipple seemed more like the point of collection for the milk than the source of the milk. He placed his mouth, tentatively, and the milk actually tasted like milk, well it was milk, he remembered, but it tasted like cow's milk. It also tasted like tears. He pressed her breast into his mouth and then squeezed a drop out. The milk began to pour our faster than he could drink and he was swallowing and gasping and then he had trouble swallowing quickly enough. His mouth filled and then the milk began to trickle down the edges of his mouth.

She dropped her breast and then gave him her other breast.

He really didn't want to do this. "Can I—" he started to ask, but she said, "This one is still full."

But she must have been relieved somewhat because after a minute she said, "Why are you drinking it like that?"

He looked up at her, from the floor of the women's bathroom. "What do you mean?"

She rubbed his upper lip. "You have a damn milk mustache. You're drinking me like a milkshake."

He stood up, his legs asleep from having knelt for so long. "What am I supposed to do, Victoria?"

"My name is Vicky."

He washed his face in the sink. There was another knock at the door. As Victoria opened it, she said, "This thing doesn't lock."

A security guard stood in the hallway. "What's going on in there?"

"We had an emergency," Vicky said, "A health emergency."

"Pack it up," the guard said.

Ed walked out into the hallway and he could see the passengers sitting at the tables under the windows, conspicuously not looking at them but he could tell they were looking at him as the security guard led them up to the crew deck. Ed wanted to just turn then and find a janitor closet to climb in to. It was bad enough that he still had the taste of breast milk in his mouth. It was bad enough that they had been caught. It was bad enough that people had seen them. He didn't even want to think about that. But he didn't want to have to sit through their interrogation. The security guard led them into a room with a table bolted to the floor and long wooden benches around the wall. They all sat down.

"There was a complaint that a couple was having sex in the second deck bathroom."

"I didn't see anyone having sex in there," Victoria said. "Did you Ed?"

"We weren't having sex," Ed said. "It's a misunderstanding."

The security guard asked them the important questions, their names, their addresses.

"So you two live together?"

"We're married," she said. "If we had been having sex," Vicky blurted out, "to make this point clear, would we have been doing something wrong?"

"Indecent exposure. Public fornication. These are serious crimes."

"Those aren't crimes," Vicky said. "Raping someone, that's a crime."

"This is still—"

"Stabbing someone and throwing their corpse overboard, that's a crime."

"Vicky, please," Ed said.

"We reserve the right to press charges," the guard said.

"What do you think we were doing in that bathroom?"

"It doesn't matter what I think," the guard said.

"It matters to me," Vicky said. "It matters a hell of a lot to me."

"I don't want to know anything about what you were doing in the bathroom," the guard said, "but tell you what we're going to do. You two are going to ride up here back to Seattle and once our civilized passengers disembark, you two can get off—" The guard straightened the manila envelope on the desk. "—rather, disembark."

He took them into a room overlooking the top of the ship. Above them, they could see the captain in the captain's deck and the radar turning around and around. They sat down at far end of the benches. "We are convicted fornicators," Vicky said. "Crimes of passion," she said.

Ed knew it was supposed to be funny and they laughed, but as they laughed and looked out over the water it didn't seem funny. Their two shadowy reflections lay against the glass. He could see his head and the shape of his nose, a small outline floating in Victoria's much larger, even endless, expanse.

# Mirror Dress

I WALKED BY THE DRESS ten times on the way to the bus stop before I realized I liked it. I enjoyed seeing what they put on the Glamour Mannequin next, and how they arranged the clothes to make it seem natural. The short mannequin, maybe five feet tall, stood in the window of The Wrecking Yard, a consignment and junk shop. Once, she'd faced the wall and held a roll of wallpaper. Another time, they hung a kite from the roof of the display window, and she held a spool of twine in her bottom hand. Now she was in this wild dress with her arms raised like she had just twirled a basketball.

I think it might have been some '60s dance move I never knew. My parents weren't dancers. It wasn't that they physically couldn't dance. It wasn't that they didn't like music. My mother loved music, but she loved a handful of songs that she listened to over and over again. There were just very few occasions when they were even exposed to anything with a beat. One night when Eddie Rabbit was on *Solid Gold,* my parents sat together and mouthed the words to "Step by Step." My parents went for walks in the neighborhood after dinner and spent Saturday nights playing Monopoly with their friends weekend after weekend, until I thought that was what adults did on Saturday nights. Like I said, my parents just weren't dancers.

My brother danced, although he only went out onto the floor because he really liked music, not because he enjoyed dancing and definitely not because he looked good out there. I've only seen him dancing with his fiancée, late at night in a club if it's dark enough and he's had enough to drink and he's tired of playing the piano and he just wants to stand with the tired people and sway to the music. My brother and I love songs more than anything else, more than the movies, even. I don't know where we got this. Mom only has three records she listens to, Fleetwood Mac's *Rumors*, Crystal Gale's, *Crystal Gale*, and Eddie Rabbit's *Step By Step*.

Dad owned a single 45, Marvin Gaye singing "I Heard It Through The Grapevine." He used to listen to it while he stretched before his morning jog, and I'd wake up thinking about Raisin Bran. Five years ago, Dad suffered a fatal coronary embolism while running under the soccer posts on the marshy athletic field at the high school where I'd start to go in the fall. They said he must have been sprinting, because he'd kicked splatters of mud all the way up to his shoulder blades. He'd kept moving, probably walking, out onto the more solid field where he lay down and didn't get back up. I remember sitting in the hospital reading the poster, "A third of all men don't survive their first heart attack," and I wondered how many more the other two-thirds were likely to have, and I wondered why they had this reminder posted out here for a family who did know better. My father hadn't eaten a piece of bacon since I was six years old. He was an exercise freak and kept us all to his health regime. We ate Brussel Sprouts at practically every dinner. I'd never had real butter at home. I wondered sitting in the waiting room, why my father would start sprinting and what that looked like, his long arms and legs flailing up and down, and his old Nikes plowing into the soft mud on the field.

As soon as we came home, Mom threw all the low cholesterol margarine, the non-fat milk, the fake eggs into a white garbage bag. She returned home later with Land O' Lakes butter, and a fatty hunk of pork loin, AAA jumbo farm fresh eggs, and a pack of Virginia Slims. Sitting down to a breakfast of bacon and eggs, the three of us didn't even know how to ask for the salt shaker without Dad there to hear us ask.

Before James moved out and before Dad died, Mom sometimes brought home a record she'd bought during her lunch break and she'd play it while she sat on the floor in front of the stereo with her shoes off, the bag and receipt in her lap. She'd look out the window, down the block at the fir tree growing in the front strip of the green belt.

James and I sometimes sat on the couch while Mom listened to her experiments. "What if it's another *Rumors*?" she'd ask. She kept bringing records in, but no other one matched the familiarity of her favorite three records and finally James graduated from college, and he didn't sit in the living room with us. So Mom stopped bringing records home. Shortly after he left, I tried to get Mom to sit and listen to the Thompson Twins, but she said that our ritual was wrecked now that James had gone. "We'll find something new to do. A new tradition," she said.

James used to work in the hardware store where I work, but now he's a piano player, though he can also play the guitar and sing. Mostly, he plays the piano for other singers. He travels around a lot. He calls himself a good, cracker-jack player, not a great musician. He says, it's hard for most musicians to know their place in the world. He writes songs and sometimes I receive his homemade cassettes in the mail, with their neatly typed liner notes and xeroxed photos of his scowl under his silver dollar sunglasses. Once someone on Broadway in New York wrote him a letter asking if they could use his song, "The Tapioca Waltz." James called me up even though it was four in the morning and he started singing the song. "They said they'd pay me for it." I knew the song from the tapes he'd sent me a long time ago. On the tape, when he sang it, he had used this corny cowboy accent and had ended the song crying out for "some libation," but now he sang it like it was "Rhiannon" or something. It had lyrics about a childless couple dancing in their kitchen and bumping up against the white refrigerator. They adopted a Mexican boy, and the boy grew up to be a fantastic dancer and won all kinds of dance-offs, and had a fight with the parents in their kitchen and told the couple that they shouldn't dance in front of other people, particularly him, because it was like watching them do it. When the son left, they danced anyway, slowly at first, and then they really started to get going, and after a while it was like they had never stopped dancing.

"But you can't dance," I said. "Mom and Dad can't dance. We have cursed dancing genes."

"It's not that some people *can't* dance," James told me, "it's that other people don't like to watch them dance."

Maybe I liked the mannequin's outfit because she danced in it, a flashy outfit that looked like a disco ball. I stopped on the sidewalk and walked up close to the glass, where the light glanced off its metallic squares and reflected on the pane.

I didn't even think about the dress, all day, but on the way home, five minutes before The Wrecking Yard closed, I stepped off the bus and they had removed it. Now, she wore overalls and had a paddle ball in one hand; the rubber ball swayed back and forth in the window display like the pendulum that Professor Calculus always carries around in the Tintin comic books. A hanger lay behind the mannequin on the dusty plywood floor.

I yanked open the door to find the owner standing in front of it with a long necklace of keys. She smoked a cigarette and grumbled while she sorted them. I asked, "What happened to that dress?"

"We're closed."

"I want to buy that silver dress that was on the mannequin this morning," I said. "Unless you sold it."

It cost four hundred dollars. When I heard that, I just about turned around and left, but the saleswoman, who I've seen come and go from the shop with a bullet-shaped, stainless steel coffee cup, put out her cigarette and smiled at me. She said she'd sell it to me tax free. I couldn't very well change my mind anyway, because I wanted it. The woman didn't close the store because I had wanted it. I didn't know what I was going to do with it, because I knew I wasn't going to wear it. "It's a fantastic piece. You'll be quite the hit. And you've got the figure for it. So petite. You'll be a sensation." The saleswoman ran my debit card through the machine and destroyed my checking account.

I hurried home to hide the box under my bed, but Mom's Caprice Classic idled at the bus stop, sending out clouds of smoke. Sitting behind the wheel, she sucked on a cigarette and drank coffee from a paper espresso cup marked with her burgundy lipstick. Mom worked as an insurance agent selling coverage to public utility districts and spent almost a week out of every month at a conference of one type or another somewhere in the state. She was supposed to be in Omak now, so I was sort of surprised to see her. Whenever she showed up like this, I knew she hadn't done well at her conference. She would either want to perform therapeutic shopping or find a pair of dull scissors and cut off my hair. Her window purred down and the mix of power perfume—her phrase—Elizabeth Arden, menthol and extra strength pine scent car freshener spilled out onto the sidewalk.

"Do you want to go shopping?" I asked her. I held my box below her window.

"I thought we might get some coffee. Get in." She smiled lazily at me. "What's in the box?"

"Have you been driving all day? Why don't you go home and sleep?" I put the box in her back seat and lay my coat across it.

"I'll just wake up tomorrow," she said, "no matter what time I go to sleep. Why waste an afternoon?"

"What's this?" I held up the small shot cup.

"Just a couple of ounces of coffee," she said.

"Of espresso. You're wired."

"I bought it hours ago."

She leaned behind my seat, and I watched, horrified, as she pulled the box from under my jacket "What's in the box, honey?"

"A surprise," I said.

She opened it and cocked her head, jingling her earrings. She looked at me. "Is this from the hardware store? What is it?" The dim light coming through the rain covered windows filled the car with gently pulsing light. And then she pulled the shimmering dress up. "It's a dress?"

"You weren't supposed to look," I said. "I was going to save it for your birthday."

"Honey, it's not until May."

"I know," I said. "But when I saw it, I knew you had to have it."

"It's lovely," she said. She pulled the tag on the back and read the size and then held the dress up again. "You don't know my size."

"You're a seven," I said.

"You're sweet. But I'm a nine."

"You can fit into this."

"By May it might be too big." Mom was always dieting and

only bought clothes that fit on her weight trajectory. "It sure is daring," she said. "You think I could pull this off?"

"Of course you can, Mom," I said.

"If I was your age, I could definitely pull it off. Now I'm too old and fat and you're you, so no one can wear it."

"I could maybe wear it," I said.

Mom looked at me out of the side of her eyes. "We'll see about that. Kind, gentle Kim in anything that shows off her knobby knees—besides khaki shorts." She started out into traffic. I always enjoyed riding in Mom's car because she drove with lazy sweeps of the steering wheel, bringing the car to a sleepy pause at a light and then gradually easing back to speed. I couldn't hear the street traffic, just the sound of rain on the windshield, the anemic jazz on her light FM station and her repetitive monologue about the conference. I have heard before about the staged wild parties, the bad deals, and the ongoing feuds between utility commissioners. Mom usually bought a keg, bribed one of the bus boys to carry it up to the room and then gradually leaked out the rumor that Ingram Insurance had a keg and then these old fire or water or sewer commissioners came to Mom's room to party. Drawing the steering wheel around with a scything sweep of her arms, her bracelets and necklace jingled like wind chimes.

We walked across the wet parking lot to the Burke Museum coffee shop and Mom flirted with the coffee guy using her same tired line. "Cappuccino with a dollop of white froth," she said with a breathy voice.

We sat at the table by the window. Mom looked around the place at the students hunched over their gigantic text books and the beret crowd scrawling in their notebooks. "In the '60s everyone would have a cigarette burning and then the place would look like some work was getting done. At work you can always tell the shirkers. They don't smoke." Mom must have worked in the last outlaw smoking office on the planet.

"Do you want to move outside to smoke, is that what you're getting at?"

"As soon," Mom said, "as I finish my coffee." I sat at the table looking at the other people in the shop and Mom sat at the table watching me watching them.

"When are you going to get your act together?" Mom asked me.

"What kind of question is that?"

"Just trying to make conversation. I'm asking you, what are your goals and aspirations. A mom's supposed to ask questions like that."

"What aspirations do you think I have?"

"Come on. We've talked about this. I don't believe you should *do* anything. I sympathize with you, I really do. When I was young it took me a long time to figure out what I wanted to do with my life. I, myself, was a flake. I was spacey. I was out-there. Once I forgot to pay my rent even though the money was in my account, and then I got about ten days into the month and thought, wow, I have enough cash to get something. I spent two days window shopping, and then I bought these thigh-high boots I only wore once and a couple of days later I received three days notice. Evicted. I don't know what happened to those boots. I'm sure they'd look snappy with that dress you bought."

"Mom, you're telling me you wanted to grow up to be a public utility district insurance saleswoman who professionally throws keggers for fifty year old men?"

As I said that, her eyes glazed over, and she tilted her head a little, and I thought, damn, a clean hit, I sunk her battleship. She instinctively pulled out her cigarette pack and child-proof lighter and failed to light it. "You can't smoke in here," I said.

"Let's go outside then," she said. We sat on the cast-iron bench outside under a maple tree, and she smoked, and finally she said, "Your brother's getting married."

"I know."

"He won't tell me when he's getting married. Has he told you anything?"

"He didn't even tell me he was engaged. You told me."

"Yeah? I thought you told me."

"He won't tell me when he and Lorna are getting married."

"Maybe Lorna told us."

Mom always blew out her smoke with a forceful gust of air like she was trying to knock something over with the power of her breath. She blew out now, forcefully, and then looked at me. "You know, I think she did tell us. How come I always have to learn anything important about James from someone else?"

"Why don't you ask him that?" I asked, but Mom held her cigarette in front of her face and stared into the distance. She didn't even notice I had asked her a question.

At four o'clock in the morning, I woke. I lay in bed shaking because I wanted to put on the dress and do something, like go out dancing, and the lights would flash on and then the whole room would go almost dark except the spark of the dress, and the music would thrum and pump, and the lights would flash back on, and my dress would explode in blues and greens. What would I do with a dress like this? It's the kind of dress a jazz singer would wear or a wild girl would wear to a prom or a cocktail waitress in a sleazy city bar. I went downstairs to drink some water and, as I felt around in the dark cupboard for a glass, it occurred to me that I could take the dress back. Mom had left it on the kitchen table. I carried it upstairs and slid it under my bed. And then I slid it back out. The dress glowed in the darkness like a blanket covered with diamonds. I put it on and opened my closet door to look at myself in the mirror, and I slowly began to dance, not doing any of the moves I'd learned by watching the other kids at Ballard High School, but just moving slightly, so that the glittering fabric shifted and cast stars against the mirror and wall.

When I was in middle school, my brother played saxophone in a jazz band with a couple of clerks who also worked at the hardware store. At a summer party he let me sing "Baby Please Don't Go." My parents threw the party for my brother who had just graduated from college, and it was at our house, or he would never have let me sing. I stood in front of these people and sang this old song. I was there, in front of them while they asked for more jell-o salad and while they tried to scoop the last of the Heinz baked beans from the edge of their wilted paper plates, and I sang. I sang clearly and forcefully, and slowly, everyone stopped to watch me. I always wanted to go back to that stage on that summer night. I didn't realize how much I had missed that night until the following Thanksgiving when I asked James about the band and he off-handedly said, "Oh, they broke up."

"How come you didn't tell me?"

"There's a lot of things I don't tell you," he said.

His then girlfriend and years-later fiancée, Lorna, wore a sweater with glittering bead fringes at Thanksgiving dinner. Her long, two-tone red nails gave her trouble picking up the fork and knife. She cut her turkey with the knife and then set the knife lengthwise on the edge of her plate and then moved in with the fork. I had trouble understanding her because, when she spoke, she covered her mouth with her napkin. After we had finished, instead of going into the kitchen to help James and me clean up, she sat on the couch and drank coffee with Dad and watched the football game. Mom sat across from her. I heard them talking about the player's tight uniforms and butt slapping. "Doesn't that make you uncomfortable?" she asked my father and my mother laughed her evil, snarky shark laugh. My father, even though he may have been uncomfortable with Lorna, admitted that he took a guilty pleasure in the sport because of the physical camaraderie of ball players. "Myself? I'd be out on my ear if I spent as much time on the job with my hand on other men's butts," Dad said. Lorna laughed. Snickering, Mom almost regurgitated her drink. "What did Dad say?" James leaned in from the kitchen, knowing he'd missed something. Dad folded Lorna into the family, and instead of wincing when she made her jokes, we laughed.

When James volunteered to go to the store to pick up some Cool Whip, I went with him and after he told me that the band had broken up, we didn't have anything to say to each other. I realized he had never told me anything about himself. He smoked a cigarette, some foreign and sweet smelling brand, not the Camels and Marlboros the guys at the hardware store smoked. He wore a black tie made out of material that glittered faintly in the passing street lights. I expected him to ask what I thought about Lorna or even if I liked her but he'd reverted back to his cigarette and steering wheel. James drove like he was being filmed. He spent a lot of his time glancing in the rearview mirror and then taking a drag on his cigarette and leaning forward slightly to ash in the open tray.

"Lorna looks like Mom," I said. "Except Lorna is much better at doing her nails."

"Yeah?" James asked. "Mom looked twice as good at Lorna's age. What's with you?" He went through another full routine of rearview mirror check, drag, and then ash. "You're mad I didn't tell you about the band? You don't care about the things I do. We're brother and sister."

I wish that had been how it was between my brother and me, but I could've told him anything about me. I thought then sitting in the car, listening to his music, with instruments I couldn't even identify, there was nothing I could tell James about me that he couldn't imagine himself.

I took piano lessons the summer I was twelve from my brother's tutor Ms. Frost. Every Tuesday and Thursday I went to an old house on 42ND. It had a leaning fir tree in the front yard and a metal lattice bench in the shade under the boughs that hung so low over the sidewalk, people had to duck when they passed down the street. Ms. Frost sat on the bench and smoked between lessons. Sometimes, I would arrive early and listen to the lesson before me. I could hear Ms. Frost banging away at the piano and a woman singing like someone having their tonsils pulled. I don't know what kind of music it was or even if it was any kind of music at all. I thought maybe they were doing some vocal exercise. When they stopped, the piano crashed and they laughed. Ms. Frost shouted out, "Shake that thing, honey!" I could see her elbow and the lace cuff of her sleeve through the open window. Her elbow kept jostling the curtain. When they stopped, she stood up, pulled her skirt straight and looked outside at the sky. She smiled at me and then snapped the window shut.

I wanted to know what they found so funny. I stood by the bench and took out my school book and marked the place with my finger. When the woman and Ms. Frost opened the door, I pretended to read. Ms. Frost sat on the bench next to me. I could smell her perfume, a hard lemon odor. She told me to go inside and begin my lesson. She'd be in, in a minute, after she had a cigarette with Mrs. Wallace. When I went inside, Mrs. Wallace and Ms. Frost stood outside and shared a cigarette. The woman took a long drag on the cigarette and handed it over to Ms. Frost. They exhaled and talked and inhaled and talked. I took out my music book with "When the Saints Coming Marching In" and "Sweet Georgia Brown," but I wanted to play that music that you couldn't write down.

James hated to hear me practice so much that he wouldn't come home until he knew I was finished. I didn't know that until much later, but when I was a kid I was grateful to have the house to myself while I practiced. On days I didn't have my lesson, I hurried home, getting ready two periods before the end of school. I took all the things I'd need later out of my locker and then as soon as the bell rang, I walked briskly down the hallway, but not so quickly that anyone would think, where's Kim going to in such a rush, and I'd speed-stroll right out the side door.

On days when I had practice, I tried to show up as early as possible to listen to Mrs. Wallace sing and play. I didn't know what kind of music it was. It was discordant and odd. She howled or barked or made a yipping bark like my neighbor's dog Francis. Sometimes after I had finished my scales at home, I practiced playing the way Mrs. Wallace did. I mashed the keyboard with my fists. I let my hands crash on the keyboard. I pretended to type like I was in a typing speed test. I did anything to make noise with the piano, hoping I would discover how she made those kinds of sounds, hoping I'd discover the noises that Mrs. Wallace knew. I didn't want to ask Ms. Frost and I didn't know anyone who would help me make pure noise besides, maybe, my brother, but he might think I was making fun of him. I went to the library and checked out tapes of old piano songs, but I couldn't find an entire song that sounded the way I wanted it to sound. I found a moment in a long complicated piano piece that sounded close to it, and then I found Jelly Roll Morton and a single song by someone named Pine Top Smith, and I listened to them throw this shaggy rhythm out of the piano. They pounded on the keyboard like their hands were phone books. I had a whole half hour each day when nobody was home, and I would practice until the joints of my fingers felt as hollow and brittle as twisty straws. For a full hour, I'd memorize that song—and practice the boogie-woogie and stride piano, and sometimes I'd just close my eyes and play.

My world history teacher talked about how Winston Churchill used to put marbles in his mouth because Mr. Churchill, despite his skill with words and phrases, had so much trouble with the sounds themselves that they became trapped between his tongue and teeth. My fingers had trouble striking the keys the way I wanted them to, so I played with pencils jammed over my ring and middle finger, or with my fingers masking-taped together. I played with my mother's dirt-clod-hardened gardening gloves. Unable to find an isolated note through the straw- and soil-caked canvas, I hammered in the general direction of each key. Each blow echoed chromatic notes. I played the piano like a machine gun, scattering notes everywhere.

I played "When The Saints Come Marching In" so many different ways that I had it memorized. I was supposed to clean the kitchen before anyone came home and I kept forgetting about it. "What do you do all day?" Mom asked me. I'd play right until I saw my brother's car pull into the driveway, and then I'd start studying algebra at my desk and in a few minutes Mom would be home.

At five o'clock James slammed the back door and opened the refrigerator and popped a can of Coke. He'd sometimes come down the hall to the sewing room and sit at the piano and play some Mozart from his head or Beethoven or anything I'd heard about a million times before in the movies or on TV.

One day I came home and played my scales really quickly and then began playing a boogie-woogie, something I'd been working on for a little while. I started to sing like the old records. I was having a great time, and I didn't hear James open the door. He wore sweat pants and a T-shirt and wool socks. He must've been home sick. He watched me throw my hands against the keyboard. He asked me who taught me that. He said it really low-down in his throat like I'd borrowed his bicycle and popped the tire. He said it real low and I stopped right in the middle of walking the bass and turned around on the bench. "Where did you learn that?" he asked me again.

"Nowhere," I said. "I checked out some tapes from the library, you know, and just sort of worked it out." I looked at him standing in the hallway with his hair all frazzled from being in bed sick. His cheeks glowed from his fever. He pursed his lips and I waited for him to smile and laugh because I was having such a great time. I thought, finally I can have some company. He just rolled his tongue in his mouth like he'd just bitten into a super tart gummy bear. "Well it's loud and it sucks. You are the most out of control, out-of-tune, cat-in-heat sounding player I've ever heard. And I'm sick and I'm trying to sleep. So, if you don't mind, you can bust the piano into little pieces when I'm not here." He walked across the room and brushed my back with a wave of his hand to dismiss me from the bench. He began to play the Mozart piece he'd learned for recital. He played from memory with his eyes closed. I went to the window and watched how controlled he was in playing and I wished I could've played like him.

Ms. Frost had been James' teacher from the time he was thirteen until he was sixteen. She had his picture hanging in the hallway along with other students. I knew she didn't have all her student's pictures on the wall because James had a friend, Mark Finney, who had practice every day just after him, and Mark didn't have his picture on the wall. Nor did I.

My father caught me playing the piano in the spring before he died. I didn't hear him come inside the house. I had wanted to practice the beginning to a Beethoven sonata, but had ended up hammering out a sound that rang through the living room. "Whoa!" Dad yelled, "Kim. I gotta dance." My father hopped around the living room floor, throwing off his suit jacket, tossing away his briefcase, and unraveling his tie. I kept playing, and I didn't think much more about playing like James' playing or getting on Ms. Frost's wall.

Each night, after I had brushed my teeth and hair, I slid the white box from under my bed, resolved that this would be the last night I'd have the dress and that tomorrow I'd return the dress to The Wrecking Yard. The lights came from outside, and fell on the dress, which glowed and glittered like a suit of armor. I could see pieces of my face and hair in the reflective squares on the dress, each piece of my face slightly skewed. Flecks of light flicked over the walls like a cloud of firebugs swarming into my room.

One morning, in the April following my brother's engagement to Lorna, I found him in the middle of the downstairs floor with a pack of ice on his head. "Hi," I said. He wore a stained white dress shirt without a collar. It was untucked and I could see the whiter-than-white swatch of his belly fat going into the deep cavity of his belly button. He had twenty-o'-clock shadow and rolled over and groaned when I passed him.

"Kim?" he asked.

"Yeah." I didn't want to hear any of his stuff. I didn't even know he'd be coming, I was so far outside the Mom-James loop. So I stood in the entry way with my backpack, and he said, "Kim. I'm married."

"You are not married yet. Something could always happen. She could come to her senses or something." I'd talked to Lorna at length on the phone a couple of weeks ago about getting married. She liked to talk to Mom and me about James. Everything I knew about him came from these conversations.

"No, Kim, I am already married to that girl."

James sat up and looked at me standing in the doorway with my backpack. He rubbed his pouchy eyes with the edge where his wrist joined his forearm. He used to have a string puppet that would throw a punch if you pressed it. We would sit in the car going on one of Mom's insurance trips to Hamma Hamma or Walla Walla or somewhere, and James'd hold the puppet up and it would box me in the nose, and I'd grab the little ball fist and see the plastic string between the forearm bead and the hand bead.

"Don't you want to celebrate?" James uncapped a bottle. "We have plenty of liquor to see us through the day."

"I have to go to work."

"At seven-eighteen in the goddamn morning? Come on. Sit and talk to me for a second." He stumbled up and tucked his shirt in under his stomach and sucked everything in to tuck back his pockets and fasten his belt. I followed him into the kitchen. Stuff covered the counter: crushed Coke cans, an empty bottle of Bacardi, a half opened bottle of Smirnoff, and a soggy carton of Minute Maid orange juice with the cap lodged sideways into the mouth. James hefted the carton to feel the weight. "There's plenty," he said, "if you'd like a squirt." He put the cap on right and then shook the juice. He poured two doses of orange juice and then applied a shot and a half from the Smirnoff bottle.

He handed the mug to me. "Mine is the "Ingram Sales Employee of the Month," I said. "This is yours."

"Congratulations," James said.

"So when did you hitch up?"

"Weeks ago," he said. "Justice of the Peace hooked us up. But Mom, you know, missed it, so we're going to do the ceremony again and have a party so Mom feels like she's in on the whole thing."

"You're already married."

"I don't understand the whole marriage thing. It's not like there will be any surprises come wedding day. Lorna and I talked about whether we wanted to get married in complete privacy. There isn't any suspense in the whole, do you take this woman to be your lawfully wedded wife. It's a done deal once it reaches that point. Anyway, we taped it. You can watch it whenever you want."

"Some people like to be at their brother's wedding," I said.

"That is so sweet," he said. He set his cup down and wrapped his arms around me. I could smell that he had vomited and done a pretty good job of getting it out of his shirt because he smelled more like Palmolive than puke.

"Why are you so wasted?"

"Self-induced bachelor party."

"So when is this fake second marriage? Can I come or do I just get to watch the video?'

"Tonight," he said. "I think."

I came home from work and Mom was in mid-flight down the stairs. "Honey, how come you've come home so late? We have to go."

"Mom," I said, "I just got home from work."

"Why don't you change? I'll wait in the car."

I went upstairs and put on the white gown I had worn to the spring dance, with my first and only boyfriend. I hadn't known really where to take him for dinner, so I took him to the Holiday Inn which had a penthouse right on Puget Sound in Ballard. It was raining, and we had a couple of hours before the dance when I picked him up, and he was wearing this really cheesy jacket he sometimes wore in debate. It looked like the kind of jacket a young tenure-track professor might wear in a sitcom, tweedy with patches on the elbow and even the faint smell of pipe tobacco. We went into the elevator and came out into the lobby of a hardcore dance club, techno all over the place and a guy in drag looked us over and said, "You two aren't twenty-one, combined. If you're looking for a room, I'd suggest you go out to the parking lot and take care of your business because, one, it won't cost you any money, and, two, you two aren't going to take enough time to go to all the trouble of renting a room."

I peeled the gown off, balled it up, and then threw it under my bed. I pulled out the box with the mirror dress. Mom started to honk the horn. I threw it on and I ran outside. When I sat in the seat next to Mom, she said. "Honey, that dress is wearing you. You look like a toaster."

Mom rented the Oddfellows Hall in Greenwood, in North Seattle, and when we arrived, dozens of North End commissioners, fire, water, and sewer and their spouses crowded in three large clumps. Men wore acrylic rain jackets with the peeling press-on logos of utility district numbers and native woodcarvings. Beepers periodically burst, cell phones made faint machine-gun rings. The walkie-talkies squawked.

"Hello, Merrill," said a skinny, older balding man in a tight-fitting brown suit. His ring of gray-tinged hair trailed in wisps down the sides of his head. He cupped my mother's forearm and drew himself up against her in a half hug, half kiss to her cheek. And then he glanced over me and my dress and said, "You're Merrill's daughter? I'm Charles Merit. I'm very pleased to meet you." He then engaged me in one of his half embraces, half kisses. His leathery chin, covered with hard stubble, lacerated my cheek. I could smell his cologne, a deep, oily wood smell like a creosote log. He drew back from us and snapped his teeth in a wide grin. "I'm so happy for your son. And who will be next? Who will be the very next one? Which one of you will it be?"

"I'm not seeing anyone," I said.

"Well, I am," Charles Merit said. "But in your case I can

make an exception." A hard laugh forced its way out between his solid grin. He took my mother's arm and whisked her across the room to begin the rounds with the commissioners.

James walked around me and whistled low. "Mom told me about this dress. She said you bought it for her birthday."

"I bought it and she saw it. What was I supposed to say? Do you know how much this dress cost?"

"Don't tell me because I do know how much you earn a month."

"I didn't buy it for myself."

"You must have because no one else wants to look like the Death Star."

"The Death Star wasn't covered with mirrors. And it didn't have legs like mine."

"Well enjoy my wedding. Everyone will be looking at you. The Death Star with legs."

"You're already married and, anyway, they aren't looking at me. They're looking at each other and drinking the punch and pretty soon they'll be dancing and frenching each other in the stairwell. I've been to Mom's shindigs before." I poured myself a cup of punch and a man wearing a skipper's hat and a dark blue suit jacket with a red kerchief in his pocket had taken James' place.

"Who are you here with?" he asked me.

"With him," I said. I pointed out my brother who had wandered away to examine the upright.

"Congratulations, that's some wedding dress."

"I'm his sister."

I studied his face for a second. He wasn't looking at me now. He held his plastic cup of punch and stared at the ice coated with frosted sherbet. Liver spots and thick, black grout-brush wires covered his hands. A bracelet hung from one of his loose sleeves. "I have a daughter not much older than you," he said.

"She's going to the UW, rows on the crew—maybe you know her? Karen Johnson? She's going to Syracuse this fall. Smart girl. She and I see each other the first Friday of every month. We're pretty close, really. When I hear about how people get along with their daughters, I'm thankful every time I see her."

"Hi Commissioner Johnson, I need to ask my daughter a question—"

"But Mom," I said. "I was just getting into his story about his brilliant, successful daughter who, wouldn't you believe it, is my same age."

"You can talk to him later," she said. "Would you play the piano?"

"Maybe he can finish his tale, now," I said.

"Please, will you play *The Wedding March*."

"Mom, I wish you had talked to me earlier. I haven't played the piano for five years."

"It's not difficult."

"How would you know?"

"How difficult can it be? Everyone plays that song. And I didn't think it would be right to have a musician, because your brother's one and our family is full of musicians anyway."

"James hates my piano playing and I'm not going to play this march just because you're too cheap to hire a high school kid to play it."

"You want me to pay you? How much?" Mom flipped out her red leather Ingram Insurance monogrammed checkbook, cracked out her embossed fountain pen ready to write an amount. "What'll it be?"

"100 dollars," I said.

"You're just playing *The Wedding March*. This is your brother's wedding. 25."

"He's already married and I'll keep playing. 100."

"All right. 50—" and she wrote the check out and handed it to me. In the memo line she wrote, "Brat Fee."

Mr. Johnson had followed our transaction and chuckled. "Your Mom sure is something," he said. "You should count yourself a lucky girl to have a woman like that for your mother." He took a drink of his punch, leaving a ring of hardened, red sherbet over his lip. And he sat down in the back row next to Mom.

I sat down at the piano and flipped through the music book full of the essential songs. A rusted paper clip marked *The Wedding March*. I ran my middle finger over the yellowed keys. They depressed slightly and I could feel the hammers echo quietly, deep in the piano. I looked over the top of t, he upright at everyone. They were bowed and talking. One of the sewer commissioners who'd been certified through the mail so he could marry off his own brother was going to perform the ceremony. I think my mother was too cheap and she wanted to increase the party atmosphere by skipping the austere presence of a minister. Anyway, this guy had been a phone call away and she hadn't been inside a church since my father's wake five years ago. She stood in the back of the church, not really listening to my father's brothers talk about the man they had grown up with. Instead, Mom kept stepping outside to smoke through her first pack of cigarettes. James and Lorna didn't even notice Mom's absence. Dead, my father wasn't able to keep us together.

The sewer commissioner smiled and nodded at me sitting at the piano in my mirrored outfit. I could see pieces of their arms and white scalps in my dress. I hit a note and it sounded sour and spare and I glanced at the music and then played *The Wedding March*. I had a hard time playing at first. I lifted my leg to keep time, kept reading ahead, and playing as loud as I could. I glanced up and my brother and Lorna were standing in front of the room and I stopped. No one looked at me; I had been as unobtrusive as elevator music.

I waited through the ceremony, which was short and to the point. We are gathered here today, and do you take this woman and do you take this man, and I now pronounce you man and wife. It took about ten minutes because I suppose Mom didn't want anyone who had started developing a buzz from the punch to have the edge taken off.

As soon as the commissioner pronounced them man and wife, I started playing a boogie-woogie. I didn't look up from the piano, but watched the old keyboard and remembered the afternoons where I'd look out the window and listened to the street traffic in front of our house. I'd start to play and feel the piano shake under me with its own heart beat as the wood began to sweat and gasp. I forgot for a minute that there were other sounds and I just wanted to make the piano hop-up and start to dance. When I finally looked up, I saw the light had dimmed a little, but my dress cast bright specks over the walls and the dancers' faces. My mother stood, and she and Commissioner Johnson danced. The other commissioners pushed the chairs against the walls and they started to dance, too, and soon everyone danced, and no one was watching anyone else. Even my brother and Lorna shuffled together. Charles Merit boogied. It wasn't a matter of old white guys not being able to dance or me not being able to play the piano. It wasn't a matter of James not telling us that he had already been married or Mom using his marriage as an excuse to amuse her water and sewer commissioners. It wasn't even a matter of the dress wearing me or me wearing the dress. For an hour or so James and Lorna knew we cared they were married. I listened to the shuffling rhythm of shoes on the wooden dance floor and kept time on the piano and the dancers kept up with the stride of the boogie-woogie I pumped out of the up-right. Everybody shook their thing, and everybody moved.

# Earwig

In the pit of the peach I had bitten I found an earwig. I'd looked forward to eating this peach. The woman I lived with had brought it home from the produce stand she always passed on her walk from the bus stop. The peach came in its own individual carton with the fruit shape formed in clear plastic. The peach had a damp looseness to its weight. It felt heavy, not like a tomato or an apple, but as loose and as heavy as a globe of flesh. Fiber and skin. Skin because it had hair almost like a person's skin. Hence the phrase, *peach fuzz*. Skin not like my own skin with its haze of wiry and black hair. This was a young woman's skin. Unlike any kind of woman I've ever known.

The woman I live with shaves her legs, leaving scrubby calves and underarm shrapnel. I was a late bloomer in the girl department, waiting until the girls my age had begun to get under-eye-shrivel and cynicism before I made them take a second look at me and listen to me through my timid stammers, or rather because of my softly spoken lisp. I didn't mind so much, because at 16 I was covered in hair as coarse and thick as a dime store paintbrush, and by 18 I had five o'clock shadow that grew into an actual, tuggable beard by the last school bell. At an age when most boys swagger and do a hundred push-ups without straining their smile, I already had the onset of thick, hairy, wobbly middle age. I had to wait until those girls caught up with me. I had to wait a long time.

I do not get nearly enough sleep or enough exercise. I do not get enough of the basic creature comforts. I do not get enough.

What I do get I earn by performing labor, by selling my desire to do something else by the hour. The woman I live with buys fruit by the pound, and the woman I work for buys my time by the hour. All of these increments to measure my trade-in value.

I earn time wearing my not-necessarily-professional attire at my workplace where I sit in my cubicle and listen to contemporary German music with guitars and synthesizers because I enjoy the industrial sound of men uttering and screaming and cajoling in German under the guise of heavy metal music. I enjoy this because it provides a gothic movie soundtrack to my work. I sit at one desk in a row of desks that faces over the space between my skyscraper and the next tower, and the next, through a landscape of vertical faces. Sometimes seagulls soar through this space, and they are specks drifting through the unchanging matrix of lines and grids. Sea mist, too, comes up from the bay that I can just see between the buildings if I stand in several worn spots in the hallway of an office where I labor. And I do sometimes do that, five minutes out of every hour to keep my eyestrain in check, to keep my productivity up because what I do for a living, which is data entry, is not a human task, but the task of taking what is human and making it machine.

I normalize data. This is my professional designation: Data Entry Technician IV. I was the manager of this data entry unit but—predictably—in the change of management from the old paradigm to the new paradigm, I lost my place and have become subjected to the new Quality Assurance Evangelist, or as we call her the QAE. Even though she has a mustache, she believes in error-free work the way some people believe in abstinence. Error is an avoidable but inevitable human sin punishable by an eternity of flames.

There was an earwig in my peach.

I don't know how long it had been there because when I bit into the peach, through the aforementioned peach fuzz, and sat down on the chair looking out onto the patio in the dusk, illuminated by the little candles I'd lit, with a cup of hot, honey sweetened tea at my side, I thought about other peaches I'd eaten and how this peach didn't taste like the other peaches I'd eaten, and in fact this peach had a kind of woody flavor. On the next bite, I tasted a harsh chemical, acid taste, although it was clearly biological, and not a congealed pesticide wad that had lodged into the fruit. I assessed the state of my peach, and I was eating something from inside the peach at first I thought mold, and then only when I pulled out the pit and uncovered the earwig waiting in the interior folds of the peach surrounded not by mold but earwig larva bathed in slime did I realize that I had been eating earwig larva, and I dropped the peach. The earwig began to scurry away.

I took the spoon I had used to mix the honey into the tea and stunned the earwig, and then I rolled the spoon back and forth until I had crushed the earwig's exoskeleton, and I cleaned up his remains with a paper towel. I threw the rest of the peach into the trash. I drank my tea and gargled. I brushed my teeth and took a shower.

The woman I lived with came into the bathroom on some hygiene errand, then, and asked me what I was doing in the shower and I told her I was taking a shower. I didn't tell her I was taking a shower because I had eaten baby earwigs. I think she thought I was taking a shower because I wanted to get-it-on and she said it was getting late and she was turning in.

She was reading some books her bus friend had given her. She wanted to read and go right to sleep, she said. She said it slowly so that I could hear it through the whirl of water coming down in the shower. I mean I don't count on these kinds of things. "I am just taking a shower," I told her.

"What does that mean?" she asked me. "I can see and hear that you are taking a shower. You aren't being redundant are you?"

"Sometimes," I said, "a shower is just a shower." The thought then of getting-it-on, which had been eradicated completely by eating baby earwigs, now that we were avoiding talking about getting-it-on made me think about getting-it-on perhaps too much. I did have a mint-fresh mouth. But even more than getting-it-on, I wanted to tell her about the experience of eating baby earwigs and then uncovering the earwig in the middle of a piece of fruit that I had been eating. I wanted to tell her all about this, but I didn't even know how to tell the woman I lived with these things. The earwig in the exact center of the peach half was beautiful. It had a copper casing with dark blue streaks going down to the bright blue claws coming out of its back. The peach gave freely of its white, sweet, nectar infused flesh.

# Contagion

AT THE PARK EARLY SATURDAY MORNING with my daughter, Ella, I noticed a man hide a package in the park trash can. He was an older guy, looked about sixty, a square-set guy, the kind of guy I'd assume would drive a Caprice Classic, some big and powerful sedan, a Cadillac, but he had a gold Nissan, maybe a ninety-two. It didn't have a back bumper. His white hair flew everywhere. He needed a haircut. He had stubble. He needed a shave. He carried his bag over to the trashcan in the middle of the empty park. The man wore a plaid shirt, rumpled slacks, and heavy steel-toed boots. He squinted at the sun even though he had sunglasses hanging from his breast pocket. He didn't stop to put them on. He didn't even look over to me where I stood at the swing, swinging my daughter.

I pushed Ella and she swung back and then came forward. When Ella came right up to my face, she laughed, flashing the white pads on her gums where her teeth would come out when they came out, and then her face went back to her serious scowl as the swing carried her back. Ella was tired and wouldn't sleep so I was killing time until my wife woke. Ella looked like pictures of my wife as a child most of the time, but on occasion, out of the corner of my eye, I thought I saw my brother as a baby. I suppose all babies look pretty much the same, round cheeks and button nose, a tuft of thin hair. Ella oscillated between chirping joy and angry coughing fits. On weekends I looked after her.

During the week my wife, Emma, took care of Ella while I worked a contract job for a medical supply company and while I got home and settled down. You'd think Emma would go somewhere during the weekend. But she didn't. She kept to the house while I looked after the kid. Emma left parenting articles open on the kitchen table for me to read. I told her she should go out and have some fun with her friends. "Go out and get plowed," I said.

And she said, "I don't have to get plowed to have fun."

"See a movie," I said. "Do something."

"I will. I will," she said. But she didn't. Instead, she watched me watch the kid.

I watched this guy go over to the trash can with his crumpled brown paper sack, and he put it into the trash can and then walked back to the Nissan and got into it and drove away. You'd think, then, that'd be that.

But I was curious about it. What did he have that he needed to hide here at the park? I'll admit the first thought I had was that he was some drunk throwing away his morning bottle, hiding what he was drinking from his family, from his wife or his kids or anyone who'd get upset when they went to throw out the trash and lifted it and it, rattled with empty bottles. So he came to Sandalwood Park to throw his empty bottles away.

My father drank. Growing up he kept his bottles in odd places, like adult Easter eggs. Growing up this pressure of his to drink was the only constant thing. Everything else in our house was just let go. The grass turned to dandelions and then to blackberries. Our house turned dank in the shadow of the overgrown thicket and moss grew over the windows. A patch of fungus grew on my forehead. When my mother found this patch, she cut my hair and made me sit on the porch when the sun came out.

Even after mother finally kicked my father out of the house, the bottles still turned up, a fifth of Stoli behind the porch, a brown bottle of beer with the label eaten away by slugs under the rhododendron. I'd knock a baseball out into the blackberries across the street and go find it and find a faded brown bag with a half-drunk bottle of whiskey. When I found the bottles, I'd bring them back to the house and hide them in the basement. I had a mind maybe to try them one day. This was all my father left us. This was all that was left of him, besides the photographs in the family album mom set about destroying. A picture of my father on the pier at the lake we used to visit during summer vacation. She says, here's the day you father forgot to zip his pants back up. My father in front of the Christmas tree the day he puked up the cranberry sauce. When my mother found my stash of his bottles, she threw them out and with them went the last thing I had of my father that she hadn't taken possession of.

My daughter rode the swing up and then fell, the chains trailing after her. Her burbling chatter calmed into a white lipped pucker, which meant it was time to go.

Ella liked it if I put her on my shoulder and let her yank out what was left of my hair. I put her on my shoulders, and she yanked out what was left of my hair.

I went over to the trashcan, just because I was curious, because I wanted to see if this man was like my father. There was something reassuring about these repeated activities. A woodpecker strikes at rotting trees. A drunk hides discarded bottles. There was some order to the world.

I put my daughter back in her stroller and wheeled over to the trash can and there perched at the top of the garbage was a sack, a bottle, and I grabbed it to see what kind of bottle it was, and when I opened the bag I found a bottle of Rye, sure, but I also found a Barbie doll. I inspected the Barbie doll. It seemed normal enough. It wore what appeared to be handmade clothes. She had a blackwatch plaid dress with a little leather belt and long white boots. The doll looked clean. I smelled it, and it smelled like plastic and faintly of cigarette smoke. I gave it to my daughter. She grabbed it by the hair, and started whacking it against the side of the stroller.

When I came home my wife said, "I don't think she's old enough to have a Barbie."

She tried to take the Barbie away from my daughter, and my daughter became upset. She gave her another toy. My daughter threw it to the ground.

"She likes it."

"Where did you get it?"

"A yard sale."

This was the first time Ella really expressed a true preference for something, so my wife gave her the Barbie, and my daughter began to swing it around again by the hair.

I wouldn't have thought much about the Barbie, unless what had happened next hadn't happened. What happened next implies it was the immediately next thing that happened, but it wasn't. My wife and I went about our day. We took our daughter to the grocery store. We visited a fruit stand. We went to the beach where some people played tug of war and I hopped up to lean into the thick rope to help the losing side lose. We ate our cold fried chicken cold and our daughter drank her bottle. I wanted to drink a beer with the cold chicken but had refrained from buying one at the store. I don't really want a beer, I'd thought, and then sitting there on the beach that was all I could think about was how glorious and young it would be to sit on the beach with a piece of cold fried chicken and a bottle of beer.

When we returned home, an odd rash had broken out on our daughter's neck. "What do you think it is?" my wife asked. I shrugged. What do I know about skin diseases?

We thought it might be sun screen irritation.

But the next day it became worse and we made an appointment with our doctor and then we went across town to see him. He looked at Ella's skin and had us fill out a chart of things we'd given her, food, and medicines, and lotions.

He took a sample of her blood and sent us home.

That night our daughter did not sleep well at all. Really Ella didn't sleep at all. My wife sat awake with her until two o'clock in the morning and then woke me up. "She's still not better."

"What do you think it is?"

"I don't know what it is."

I was tired. It was two o'clock in the morning. I rolled over and said, "Hopefully she'll be better in the morning."

"I can't stay awake anymore," my wife said. "I can't keep my eyes open."

"Did you try putting her down?" I asked. But even in the dark, I knew I shouldn't have asked that. I got out of bed. I could hear then our daughter sobbing and I went into the living room where my wife had set up portable crib. Ella lay in the bluish light there and looked up at me like I could do something for her, and when I went into the kitchen to set the coffee pot going, she started to scream. "Pick her up," my wife called from the bedroom.

"But we don't know what's she's got."

"You need to pick her up," my wife yelled. "I can't sleep with her screaming herself to sleep."

I picked her up, and her screaming subsided to a kind of sobbing, and then about an hour later she fell asleep. Let me tell you, an hour from two o'clock, actually by that time it was more like two-fifteen to three-fifteen in the morning, is a long time. We live in, to be honest, not that great of a neighborhood. Most times I can hear car doors slamming. Someone drunk off their ass in their house yells "woo-hoo" over and over again. Engines rev. A stereo plays in the distance. We used to live in a quiet place but my job took us away from the city for three years and when we came back this was the only place we could afford to live. But in the middle of the night it was quiet. I could hear the wind outside in the bushes growing along side the house. The bamboo chimes sang. I took her out onto the porch to drink my coffee. While I sat on the steps, a couple wearing white pants and white jackets and white panama hats and white sneakers walked by the front of the house. In the street light, the light of the moon, their white outfits almost made them look marked somehow. Quarantined.

"Howdy," the man said.

His wife looked up at the tall poplar growing in a yard a couple houses down. "Nice night," she said.

"Wouldn't know," I said. "Daughter's not feeling too well."

"Something's going around," the man said.

The next morning, as soon as Ella stirred, I rocked her and when she started to fuss, I changed her diaper. Her whimpering kicked into sobbing that I finally got to subside after rocking her until my arms ached. When she woke, I fed her a jar of pureed peaches and then some apple juice. She spilled the juice over her bib and it soaked into her sweatshirt. I was tired and when I picked her up and rocked her she fell asleep on my shoulder. I lay her down in her crib. I lay down on the floor beside the crib. Later in the morning when my wife finally woke, she found me sleeping at the foot of the crib with Ella sleeping in a sweatshirt damp with apple juice. Emma shook me awake.

"Why didn't you change her?"

"She was asleep. It's no big deal."

"Her clothes are wet."

"She's sleeping. Her clothes will dry."

"When were you planning on changing her?"

"It's no big deal."

"It's neglect is what it is. It is the same," Emma said, "as the mold you had a growing on your forehead."

I didn't know what to say to that. When she said that, my cold bedroom with the blackberry vines pressed up against the back window came back to me. Emma was saying that being raised in the house with a drinker had somehow destroyed me. Somehow as a parent, I could not help but behave in suspect ways.

I stood up and watched Emma changing Ella. Her rash had spread into a dense cluster of hard, red bumps.

"What do you think it is?" my wife asked.

"I don't know," I said. "I hope it's not contagious."

That did not win any more points from my wife. But what good would it do if we caught it and then we were bed ridden as well? Who would look after her if that happened?

"Maybe it is something in her room?" I asked. I said this so that I would have something to do, and my wife could look after our daughter.

I took all of her clothes, bed sheets, and stuffed animals to wash them and hung them out on the clothesline in our overgrown lawn behind the house. I took the bucket and filled it with hot soapy water and then washed all of her toys.

Taking the clothes off the Barbie, I found under the fabric, that the plastic Barbie skin had been marked with hundreds of cuts. It looked like maybe someone had taken a razor blade and made cut after cut after cut into the Barbie. The fabric on the back of her clothes had a sort of handwriting on it written in powdery brown ink.

I wanted to show my wife this. But I had brought the Barbie into the house. I had taken the Barbie out of the trash. I had given the Barbie to our daughter. Maybe the Barbie wasn't responsible for what had happened to her? It was superstition to make the connection, really, between the two just because they had happened on the same day. The disease could have been in her immune system for who knows how long.

I wrapped the Barbie in a plastic bag and drove to the park. On the way to the park I passed the little state liquor store beside the grocery store. I went around the block and parked in front of it. When I went inside the air conditioner filled the place with cool air. Posters for local plays and concerts covered the corkboard behind the cash register. I always meant to pick up tickets to a play. I thought about the year my wife and I had a gift subscription to the Contemporary Theater and we went out and had drinks late at night at a bar with a black marble counter. I didn't smoke, but that night I bought a pack of cigarettes and smoked them one after another until I got sick. All of that was gone now. The freedom to do stupid things had ended with Ella's arrival. I bought a fifth of Jack Daniel's and grabbed the blunt bottle by the neck, crushing the bag around it. I drove to the little park at the top of the Piper's Creek Watershed. It had a little plaque showing salmon runs and all of the streams that ran into the big stream. It was a watershed right in the middle of the city. I drank the bottle until a steady, thick warmth coated my skin. I walked over to the bigger park. I had never been there without my daughter before. And walking now down from the upper part of the park down past the swings and slide set, I felt the mothers and the babysitters lean forward to look at me and check me out to see if I was looking for a stray child. They watched me out of the corner of their eyes and I must admit I did the same thing when I saw a man walk through the park. It is only common sense. I stopped then and placed the bag with the Barbie and bottle in it in the trashcan and then walked out the other side of the park knowing they were now wondering what I'd thrown away.

When I came home my wife said, "Where were you?"

"I took our daughter to the park." I said this in a kind of automatic way, not really thinking about it, because I had been at the park and then after I said it, "I went to the park."

My wife looked after me as I sat down the sofa.

"She'll get better," my wife said.

"I hope so," I said.

My wife and I sat on the couch listening to Ella breathe, amplified and cut with static through the baby monitor. I had vowed not to repeat the mistakes of my parents and as I listened to Ella's ragged sobbing I thought I might not, I might not repeat the mistakes of my parents. Why repeat those mistakes when I could make new ones? I almost laughed then and told my wife this, but she was staring at the monitor, and listening to Ella's faint breathing as if she was a long way off.

# Randy

RANDY'S MEN HAD MOVED TO SEATTLE in the last year. They didn't know each other. They didn't spend time with each other after work. Instead they reported to the moving company where the vans were parked at five in the morning, which was not early for them. It was right on time. They had spent their lives at early morning jobs before they found Randy. They had worked at industrial farms in Utah and Idaho driving forklifts. Several of Randy's men had been bikers before they became convinced of the moral ability of their leader and found Randy on the road. Others found Randy in twelve-step programs, sheets of paper tucked into their Bibles by another of Randy's men. Some of them had found Randy in prison. When Randy came to them, they were ready for Randy and Randy knew the things that settled their world-weary souls and provided them a point of truth in an otherwise senseless and, well, mean-spirited world.

Randy lived in a cave at the edge of Montana and Wyoming in a desolate region of broken rock. His men know his story. Randy had been like them; a down-and-out tramp who'd spent nights on concrete; divorced from a woman who now had a college education and a job in an office park; dependent on menial jobs that in no way honored his capacity to think analytically; addicted to a string of corporate drugs: caffeine, nicotine, glucose, heroin. All drugs are corporate drugs, Randy said; you think if there is money to be made someone isn't making some money? A killer picked Randy up on Interstate 90 just outside of Ellensburg, Washington, tortured him and threw him for dead in a ravine in Montana. A favor was done to him that day, a favor to us all. Randy managed to survive in that ravine where he lay bleeding and broken. He lived on moss and the dew pooled in the rocks, and then finally climbed to the interstate and made his way to town and began to work as a handy man for a Christian church there and that was when he began to save other lost men like himself.

Randy instructed his men that his image, his physical presence, was not significant for the truth he had to tell them. A slight man, crooked from the injuries he sustained from the killer, his skin wrinkled and folded from his hard life, he did not make much of an impression. He seemed as substantial a person, as meaningful, as a flake of carbon drifting out of a bonfire.

Randy's men knew the sound of his voice rapidly talking about the preparation they needed to make for the new order. Soon there will be a global state. The only way to save us, Randy said, is to shock the people out of their complacency. We must get them to put down their Big Gulps, and force them into action!

In Seattle, Randy's men didn't know each other, but they all knew they knew Randy and that Randy knew them. They had come from different places, tough spots to be sure, and had found Randy when they needed him most. Sleeping off a bender in a ranch barracks before going back to a twelve-hour day, someone leaned down and handed him the slim silver booklet, *Randy's First Death*. He rose to liberate us from our corporate oppression, it said, and at first they just shook their heads. This is some nut job. And then they read the book, and next time they were drunk or fried or stoned, they found the booklet folded in their jeans jacket pocket. They would make the trip into the region of broken rock to visit Randy. All of these men had visited Randy. It was from Randy one way or another they had received the word they had a calling in Seattle. They had a paycheck waiting for them, and when they reported for work they knew that there was more to the work than showing up sober to the Elliott Bay Speed Move Co.

They found places to live among Randy's people in Seattle. They were not even aware that everyone at Speed Move Co. knew Randy. Men from everywhere worked for Randy and they might not all be white, down-and-out workers, but might be Mexican-American, or African-American, or Canadian. They might be businessmen who'd been broken down in the corporate machinery and streamlined in the last decades of the twentieth century. They might be meat packers closed out of work because of a lost thumb. They might be computer programmers who had lost the ability to write up-to-date code. They came from everywhere. They had all been homeless at one time or another and never had a job as meaningful as they had at the Elliott Bay Speed Move Co. This was a good job. It started early. It ended early. They did the bulk of their work before rush hour started around 7:30. They fanned across the city to move office furniture out of busted Internet start-ups, boxes of forms into the Military Entrance Processing Center, discarded computers, everything that needed moving from one place to another. No one talked about Randy. No one said anything outside of work. In their off hours, they trained. They followed the school buses around the city on their end-of-day routes.

At home they read their manuals and studied the writing of Randy from the Xeroxed and stapled Bible that arrived in the mail. They learned the secret language Randy spoke.

For months they drove the trucks learning to enjoy the city and their lives out beyond the mountains, not quite at the sea but close. A few of Randy's men began to resent their obligations to Randy—they liked the paycheck, sure, they liked the rent in the White Center apartment to be paid, definitely, but they decided that maybe they wouldn't read the literature anymore. Maybe they would stop learning the bus route for Jackson Elementary. A phone rang in the middle of the night, and if they didn't answer, a keeper knocked on the door. A man in a plaid work shirt, oversized blue jeans hanging by suspenders, faded and worn from hard labor, came to the door and handed them a sleek metallic cell phone. Randy was on the line speaking in his secret language. They had to listen carefully and then they nodded and handed the phone back. And they stayed in line waiting for the day to begin when they paid back their obligation to Randy.

One morning when they showed up, the door to the Elliott Bay Speed Move Co. was closed. A large sign that said *Randy* was hung over the building next door and the friends of Randy went over there. A man stood at the door and asked the drivers as they came up, Are you looking for Randy? If the person said, "Yes," then they would ask it again in the secret language and those who understood passed into the hallway where several rented vans waited. They climbed into the vans.

The drivers of the vans handed out Colt .45s and magazines of ammunition. That was all they needed. They wore the Colts once they had slid the holster onto their belt. In their uniforms, they looked like security guards.

Today we ask you to meet your obligation to Randy, the man said. They understood what they had to do because of the passage in *Randy's Second Death*. They understood what they had to do this day. They had to spill blood to make the world clean.

They drove at the speed limit down the highway to the school bus barn. The school bus barn wasn't far from the Elliott Bay

Speed Move Co. They drove into the parking lot and parked. They rushed through their familiar practiced drill inside the building and quickly paired off against the bus drivers and then once they each had a driver, the van drivers circled the building to make sure they had everyone. Then they each lowered the drivers to the ground. "Randy says put your arms under your stomach." And the drivers, the old women with their hair in buns, the young women drivers with crooked teeth and broken eye-glasses, the fat men in cardigans and comb overs, all of the poorly paid drivers were somewhat afraid; they did as they were told. Some of them were relieved, though, because then they wouldn't have to pick up the little cretins today. They all lowered themselves to the ground and then Randy's men put bullets into the groove of their spine and skull. It wasn't a precise sudden noise but a half-minute or so of noisy pops and the smell of powder as the pins snapped into the primers. It filled the barn with a flinty, serious odor. The odor of work. They went out to the buses and picked the bus route they had studied and driven many times over the last couple of months and drove. They had driven at dusk to emulate the dawn light of the live run. They followed the buses and learned the kids. There was the girl with the long stringy hair and her chubby friend in the checkered coat. There was the gaggle of kids in sports jackets and loose jeans. There was the tiny boy in the puffy jacket with the oversized earphones. They collected all of the children and after the last stop, headed out of town at the speed limit, passing over the floating bridge on Interstate 90. They pulled into the parking lot at the Luther Burbank Park and transferred the children to three waiting tour buses.

The men who had driven the tour buses climbed onto the roofs of the school buses and sprayed the school buses gray.

The children, however, were confused and not really alarmed because even though they had seen the holsters, they had seen a lot of holstered guns in their lives. The drivers told them the school district was taking them to a surprise concert. Who? They wanted to know. Who will we see? Are we going to be on cable?

They didn't tell us.

The children didn't complain when Randy's men crammed them into the three waiting buses. Three kids had to share a seat, if they could fit. Is there going to be another bus? They asked the driver because there weren't enough seats.

It won't be a long trip.

The oldest boy named Peter sat at the front of the bus. He had been held back a year, but no one held it against him. He had been held back because his parents had home schooled him but they hadn't done the things they were supposed to do, so he had a year to catch up. The other kids didn't really know he was a year older and instead thought he was a little smarter, a little bigger than the rest of them. The teachers knew. But the teachers weren't on the bus.

Peter asked the driver, "Where are we going?"

"We are going to Heaven," the driver said. "Where we will wait for Randy."

"Is that past North Bend?" Peter had not heard of a place named Heaven past North Bend, but the names of the places past North Bend were odd to him, Ashal Curtis, Tallapus Lake, Cle Elum. And then there were those two corny city names, George and Martha, Washington. Someone could have named their city Heaven, and it would be a good joke. How are things in Heaven today?

They drove then up I-90 and when they got to North Bend, they drove toward the North Fork of the Snoqualmie and onto a county gravel road. "Who are we going to see?"

"We will be there soon."

They bumped through the clear cuts and then they finally

parked the buses under a stand of trees. This stage had provided the most trouble for the planners.

The planners decided not to use fire or bullets. Instead they decided to gas the children. They caulked the doors of the buses and filled the buses with chlorine gas made from ammonia and bleach bought by the pallet from Costco. The children died—not a scar on them. They aired out the buses and lay the children under the trees. This was perhaps the most desirable option because it would provide for a kind of shock to discover these children merely dead lying in neat rows in the managed forest of fir trees.

Once the plan was completed, Randy's men climbed into the buses and drove to the mountain pass where the interstate crossed into a different climatic zone. They changed to cars, and then at Easton, they boarded a small plane that flew them to Idaho where they would walk into the region of broken rock to meet with Randy. By the time they arrived in the mountains, the authorities were beginning to put together what had happened.

The news lagged further. The school buses didn't turn up at the appointed time. It took an hour to put a police helicopter up because they didn't want to divert a traffic copter. The news would be all over it and they wanted to have something to tell them. Before they said anything, they needed to know what had happened. When they found the buses in the late morning, they let the news know—they had to at this point—and by the late afternoon they were puzzled not to find anything. The children had disappeared. There were interviews with bewildered and grief stricken parents, the image of the tense superintendent of the schools, an address by the mayor standing before the black wall of the Vietnam Memorial, a response from the governor— concert plans for a concert, "Give us Our Children Back," was organized for the next day—and then as a drizzle began to settle over Western Washington, a dirt biker found the field of dead children. Their children had not been abducted en masse by disgruntled and separated parents or a sex offender eager to stock his underground bunker with a wide assortment of grade-schoolers, or slavers shipping the kids off to cyberporn sex pens in Arkansas, but rather this was a garden variety act of terror. Who could do this? Why would they do this? What could they hope to accomplish? And when, they wanted to know, would it happen again?

# Dry Farming

AUNT GABIE CAME BACK FROM SOMEWHERE, my parents weren't even sure where, and she bought five acres of land without water rights and installed a new fabricated home on a foundation of field stones about fifteen miles outside of Ephrata, which was itself a hundred miles from nowhere. As a lost daughter returning into the family fold—despite the distance, Gabie now lay within driving distance and had an address—Aunt Gabie had some demands. She wanted, for instance, my brother, Damon, and me to go out there in the middle of the desert and spend some time with her daughter. Damon said. "But we don't know her." My brother wasn't shy, but then he didn't like strangers either. He didn't want to go out there and I wasn't looking forward to it myself.

"You don't know them," Dad said, "because you've never spent any time with them. This would be the start. Your aunt is like your grandma, only younger."

He said this as if that made everything all right. "We never spent any time with them because we didn't even know they existed," Damon said. This wasn't exactly true. We knew all about Dad's bad sister, Gabie; we just didn't think she'd ever turn up.

When my parents took us out there, they first delayed it by visiting Grandma's house near the reservoir in Ephrata. Grandma's yard had thick green grass and a huge, gnarled chestnut tree with deep, shadowy cool recesses in its canopy. The sprinklers ran at dusk, laying cold mist clouds around the porch. Everyone sat on the porch with all the doors to the house open to cool it out after the day's heat. We watched moths flit down from the sagebrush hills and bounce against the bulb. They fluttered to the porch boards. My brother and I shared a large bottle of Grandma's homebrewed root beer. The black fluid tasted bitter, faintly medicinal, but we enjoyed it because it had a little alcohol in it and so was officially forbidden and so rationed. Grandma left it to brew in an ancient black cask in the basement full of spider webs. Blackwidows lived in her house. Once one crawled up the drainpipe and into the bathtub, where it scaled the silver tub stopper chain. It had a round abdomen that was as black and shiny as marble shot with an hourglass-shaped splotch of red. The root beer, coming from such a place, didn't last long. When we got our hands on a bottle, we took turns opening it. The cap came loose with a pressurized pop and the sarsaparilla smell lifted from the glass lip. The official opener, once the cap went, took a drink and then handed it off. I held the heavy bottle for a minute considering the relation of the sharp taste in the back of my gums with the weight in the shiny black glass bottle.

My grandmother had on her old Hank Williams records. She had lots of old country records. "Don't care for Western much," she said. This sentiment was pretty much against the gospel of Ephrata, and Grandma enjoyed this about her position in Ephrata, teaching grammar to everyone's kids in the middle school but also not quite belonging among the farmers, Grant County lawyers, all the people who had lived there since the city began to prosper with the Grand Coulee dam.

Grandma didn't have any opinion about Aunt Gabie showing up or at least no opinion she would share with my parents while I was listening. While we sat on the porch and Dad asked her questions about where his sister had been all of these years, the only thing Grandma would say was that it was wonderful to finally spend some time with her granddaughter. Dad had told Mom all kinds of stories about Aunt Gabie. She used to work as a go-go dancer at a road house—that's a place where bikers and truckers and other people who live on the highway like to go to relax—outside of Coeur d'Alene. She met her husband Miller there. Miller had owned a restaurant, but they snorted through all of his money—they took a drug called cocaine and instead of smoking it like marijuana they sucked it up into their nostrils, and it cost a lot of money for just a little bit—and they came to live with us before I was born. Finally Dad kicked them out of our house. I don't remember them being there because I was just a baby. Dad always said that company is like garbage. Both begin to stink after three days.

"Dad said," Damon said, "that Aunt Gabie is just like you, only younger."

"Dad didn't say that," I said. "Damon is practicing how to tell stories."

My grandmother looked at Dad. Her eyelids drew down half way over her eyes, like she needed to cut down on the amount of light getting into her brain so she could use the rest for thinking.

"I didn't say that," Dad said. "I did say she's pretty like you. I said that."

Damon made a grunting noise, a soft burr at the back of his throat, as he stood up. He took the empty bottle with him and went into the house.

Dad and Mom talk about everything and I listen to everything. Nothing is off limits according to them. You could have asked me anything and I was liable to know something about it, something a lot of kids my age wouldn't know because their parents were stuck up—I did have a hard time believing grandma was a prude but she *was* old—and my parents were free and felt it was in my best interest to know as much as possible about the world, or I was liable to get hurt. I needed to have the facts at my disposal.

They hadn't heard from Aunt Gabie until she had called Dad and talked him into us staying with her. She was landed now, she said. She had put her wild days behind her where they belonged, she said. "Everyone needs wild days to put behind them," she said and went on to say, "I have so many wild days, I could give you some of mine. My husband is a businessman and we will pretty soon be rich farmers. We've got everything but family to come over."

We drove out the next morning from Grandma's to visit my aunt and her husband, Miller. They were doing something called dry farming—which they had to do because they didn't have the rights to any of the water on their ranch. Although my aunt had a reputation for pulling a scam or two in her time, it seemed like she was the one having a scam pulled on her. Miller was balding and wore Western shirts with the pearl buttons and worked as a mechanic on foreign built automobiles—mostly Japanese. "Problem with Miller," Dad said, "is that he thinks he can just buy the tools and having the tools means he can do the work. He has a house full of books and just because he owns them doesn't mean he's read them and just because he's read them doesn't mean he really knows what's in them."

When we arrived at my aunt's place, Miller came out to meet us. The house sat at the edge of a wide drive, circling the only lawn that could be seen anywhere from that point on the face of the earth. Beyond the patch of lawn with the scraggly fruit tree growing in the middle, its leaves already wilted, there were just boulders, sagebrush, piles of gravel, which was pretty much all there was in the prairie. This was rattlesnake country, and my brother and I were afraid to go out into the dust because we imagined the snapping of the crickets were really the rattling of rattlesnakes. Crickets flew everywhere as we got out of the car. The place smelled like dust. The dust came from miles away, thin trails of it whipped past in the wind. A breeze or wind always blew in the prairie. It blew over the slight hill and then down to the creek bed that only filled with running water when the snow melted in the spring. Miller found out he didn't even have the right to the snow on his property. Even if he could figure out a way to keep the snowmelt on his land, he had no legal right to keep it.

Miller showed us his Toyota truck. "An amazing product of the machine age," Miller said. It seemed that the entire truck had just appeared or been stamped out of some kind of truck substance rather than being assembled from a heap of parts. The house too seemed like it had come just the way it was. We followed him into the house, which smelled inside like baking bread. Aunt Gabie was in there with her daughter, Amy. Amy had long black hair, and she was so thin the bones her chest showed like ladder rungs. She wore a very tight red T-shirt and brand-new blue jeans. She was fourteen, just two years older than me and a full five years older than my brother. When she saw us, she rolled her eyes.

"Welcome to 'The Ranch,'" Amy said. Her mother didn't notice the way she said this and asked everyone if they wanted something to quench their thirst. Aunt Gabie asked Mom about the trip out and then she asked if we would like the grand tour, so we all shuffled around the house while my aunt turned on lights and opened curtains to show the view, a view really of nothing except rocks and sagebrush and the blue horizon which was really a kind of view, because rarely does anyone live in a place that has so much of a view of nothing. Aunt Gabie had shiny black hair and a ruffled turquoise blouse on that looked like a fake plastic leaf. My aunt waited until Dad and mother made the appropriate comments about her antique chest, about her bookcase full of rare first editions that weren't reading copies but an investment, about her real polar bearskin on the floor in her and Miller's room. When Mom finally said, "This is a very nice place. I am envious of your beautiful home," Aunt Gabie called off the grand tour and took everyone's orders for drinks.

"Decaf?" Mom asked.

"Sanka?" Aunt Gabie asked.

"Cream," Mom said. "Sugar."

"I'd like leaded," Dad said.

"Instant okay?"

"If you can spare the water," Dad said. My aunt didn't laugh. Miller acted like he didn't hear Dad. He began pulling coffee mugs down from the shelves in the kitchen, inspecting each one to see how clean it was. After he said that, Dad looked at Mom and then shrugged. Dad always said the wrong thing, and this was definitely the wrong thing, but he was the older brother and older brothers said things like this to their younger brothers and sisters. Aunt Gabie looked at him. "Did you bring some water?"

"What do you mean by that?" Dad asked her.

"Because we don't have water out here," she said.

"I heard that. I heard you were *dry* farming."

"You think we don't have any running water?" she asked.

"I don't know," Dad said.

"We have our own water for personal use," she said. "We just can't irrigate with it. Drinking water is fine. We can take a fucking bath if we want. Irrigation of crops is entirely something else all together."

She handed him the instant coffee, and Dad drank and made one of his dumb faces—if you didn't know him you'd just think he was burping or something—to let Mom know he hated instant coffee, but was drinking it anyway.

They drank the coffee, and then Miller took us out back and showed us the perimeter of their land. A weathered fence skirted his acreage. Three lines of rusted barbed wire held up the bleached silver and splintered posts, and it didn't seem clear to me what held the wires up besides habit and the fact that Miller called it a fence. A few half-starved steers wandered up from a yarrow—that's cattle country talk for a gully—and passed over the trembling wires. It vibrated up and down the hillside as they walked over it. The cattle lowed at us and Miller shooed the cowering animals away.

At every clack of stone or startled cricket, Damon stopped walking and put out his hands like he was balancing on a very tall, thin wall. "Do you hear that?" he said. "Snakes?"

"You want to find some snakes?" Miller asked Damon. Damon looked around when he said that.

"I'll find you some snakes, if that's what you want to find. That's the one thing we know how to farm on this farm, that'd be snakes. This is a damn rattlesnake ranch is what it is. I've even thought about that. Selling snake meat to one of those exotic meat butchers. Selling crickets might make a buck or two, too."

Damon turned around and almost started to walk back to the house, but he'd have to walk alone through a half mile of sagebrush, loose sand, and rock. I could see him looking back at the roof of the place, then he finally turned around to follow us.

At a tall pile of stones where the fence looped back around the edge of the hill and the slope dropped into a canyon, we could hear snakes. The rattle of the snakes was unmistakable, a high, fast shake like gravel in a plastic cup that slowed down and then started all over again. It came out of the pile of boulders and Damon stood way back, looked behind him and checked under his shoes just to make sure he wasn't standing on one.

Miller climbed up onto the pile. "Do you want to see them?" he asked.

"It's all right, Miller," Dad said. "You can let them be."

But once Miller heard the snakes he had to get them out of the pile of rocks. He grabbed a stalk from the ground and then squatted down in a wide opening between the stones.

"You'll get bit," Dad said.

"Snakes respect authority," Miller said. "They're reptiles and that's how things work in their kingdom."

Miller noticed then that Damon was looking away, that Damon was doing everything he could not to look at the pile of rocks. "Come over here and help me, son," he said. Damon shook his head. "There's going to be a real beauty in here. I can hear it. Can you? Come on up, kid."

I was just about going to say, "I'll help you out," so that Miller would get off his back, but then I thought how Damon could be a real baby sometimes and he was big enough now, so I didn't say anything. Damon just started to walk away.

By this time, Miller was jamming the stick into the holes of the pile of rocks and the rattling grew louder, but nothing really happened. His prodding with the stick turned into serious, deep thrusts of the stick and then his arm up to his shoulder disappeared in the pile of stones. His face turned color, except for the very tips of nose and ears. At last he flung the stick into the canyon, jumped up onto the pile of stones and began rolling them into the dry creek bed until finally he had all of the stones gone and there weren't any snakes. This seemed to piss him off even more. "Where are they?" he yelled.

We went inside, and Mom stood up when she saw us. "It's time we left, honey," she said to Dad.

"You're going so soon?" Aunt Gabie asked.

"We appreciate you taking the boys," Mom said.

"Anytime," Aunt Gabie said. "Hope you liked the place."

"I do," Mom said.

"You can come around whenever you feel like. We don't keep it locked, and you don't even have to knock, just come right inside and fix yourself a cup of coffee."

"It's really a splendid place," Mom said.

"Don't go," my brother said. He was standing there in the middle of the room like he was going to cry or something if they left. I mean I understood my brother and usually his being so sensitive was something I sort of liked, because he at least always knew how I felt and sometime his just knowing that made everything all right but right now it only made me wish that my parents were taking him with them so that I didn't have to look at his big, damp eyes.

"We made these plans a long time ago," Dad said. "And you don't know your cousin Amy and your aunt and uncle. It's time you got to know them and they got to know you." Dad looked at me. "You watch your brother, okay?"

I was already watching him, and I didn't like what I saw.

"He'll be fine once you guys are out of sight," Aunt Gabie said. "Go on. Enjoy yourself."

We watched them drive away and then it was just the brightly lit house in the impossibly bright and sunny land that was so dry our hands began to hurt. Amy had an extra bike, so she rode on Miller's bike. We rode on her bikes. There was just the wind in our ears and the sound of crickets all around us.

My brother kept saying, "Rattlesnake."

Amy was older than us and in many ways seemed like yet another aunt because she'd grown up in city playgrounds and when she spoke she had a kind of double meaning to everything she said. That she was friendly at all to my brother and me was something we couldn't understand. Rather than providing a source of comfort, it actually made us even more afraid of her. Unlike her family, our family didn't have any secrets. We had been raised in a kind of wind chamber of things that would normally be kept secret in most families. We knew things about Amy that perhaps she didn't know herself. We didn't quite know that, although I think my brother and I were aware that our open naiveté was probably the only thing we had over her. She made it clear she was the kind of person you had to have something over.

"Do you like it here?" my brother asked. He rode behind her.

She wore bright white tennis shoes and had a red ribbon tied around her white neck. She rode with her butt off the seat sort of like she was jogging. "I hate it here. This is worse than Hell, but it doesn't matter. We won't stay here. If this is a farm, how can we grow anything in the dust? Dad says this is America's breadbasket. Who wants to live in a basket?" She turned off the road, then onto a sandy little trail. The trail was very smooth and hard and covered with earth as fine as talc that lifted up as we passed and hung in the air. About five feet up, the wind caught it and blew it away.

The dust kept getting in my eyes, little grains of sand and flecks of grass. The trail ran along the very top of a ridge and the sides fell down on either side and fell down even more the further out we went until finally we were at the end, a lookout over the vast prairie between Ephrata and Othello way to the south. We couldn't even see Othello, just the prairie all brown dust and greenish sage brush fading finally to a kind of black and bluishness. The only thing in all of that space was a small farm in the valley below us with a windbreak of poplar trees. There was a road up to it and a car driving toward it, kicking up more dust. We could only hear the sound of wind in the grass and crickets snapping past us.

"Aren't you afraid of rattlesnakes?"

"I wish one would just bite me and put me out of my misery," Amy said. "If I had a rattlesnake," she said, "I'd stuff it down my pants."

She jumped off her bike and then sat down on a rock at the edge of the lookout. "Let's find one." Way below the lookout there was a rusted and wrecked car.

"Come on," she said. "Are you scared?"

"This used to be a road," my brother said. "And it stopped here."

Amy looked at him trying to figure out what he meant by that and because she couldn't she just turned and then looked at the distance. "You can't see anything from here. This is the one spot where you can really see something and what is it? Nothing. Come on, let's find us a snake."

She turned over rocks and rolled them down the hillside. "You can find anything if you look hard enough," she said.

"Stop," Damon said.

"What are you scared of?" she asked him and she began throwing rocks down the hillside. They rolled and the further down they got, the more rocks and sticks and stray bushes they picked up until they finally piled up way down below us. "You don't have anything at all to be scared of. They have rattles like babies and they make noise to scare you away because they're scared themselves."

"Please stop," Damon said.

"Are you a little girl, boy?"

"Stop it," I said, but that's all I did. Damon was shaking a little and she'd kicked up a bunch of dirt that was getting blown around in the air, but whatever had seemed to work her up sort of left her now and she sat down really quickly in the mess she'd made of the hillside. We sat there with her, thinking of things to say to comfort her. She didn't seem to be uncomfortable, but after she spoke it only seemed appropriate we could say something to her to make her feel better. Or maybe change the subject.

"Do you ever hear from your brother?" I asked her.

"Do I what?" she said. She turned to me and looked at me.

"Your brother—"

"I don't have a brother."

"You don't know about your brother?" I asked. "You had a baby brother. But before you were born your mother gave him up for adoption. You didn't know that?"

"No," she said. "No one ever told me that."

"People shouldn't keep secrets," my brother said. "That's how bad things happen."

"What else do you know about him?"

"Your mother was pregnant from she doesn't know who and so she decided to give the baby up rather than keep him because she was so young. Although, she wasn't as young as our mother when she gave birth to my brother."

"What did he look like?"

"Like a little baby."

"Have you ever seen him?"

"No."

She stared out over the space then at the clouds and the fading light. The clouds left large gaps and their undersides were dark and gray and the topside of the clouds, which we could see through the breaks, were silvery and pink from the lowering sun.

"Do you want to go down to the car?" Amy asked us. We walked down to the car and in the car we sat in the back seat and

Amy told us that this was the only place in the entire place of Hell that she could stand.

While we ate dinner, Amy didn't say anything. Aunt Gabie served us our entire portion and then we circled our hands and said grace, something we did at Grandma's house but didn't do in our own house. I always kept my head up during grace at Grandma's house to let her know that I didn't believe in God, but here I lowered my head and even closed my eyes the way Amy and Aunt Gabie did. I had Amy's hand and her fingers felt cold. They trembled in my hand and then when grace ended, she took her hand and folded it up and placed it on top of her napkin. Every time Aunt Gabie did anything, Amy turned to look at her. At one point, Aunt Gabie asked Amy, "What? What is it?"

"Nothing," Amy said.

I offered to help with the dishes, but Miller took Damon and me into the living room to show us his collection of bottle caps. He had them fixed to velvet-lined boards and they were all in a big case behind the stereo. We could hear the wind outside, a sound as steady as the air rushing over the car as we went down the freeway. Inside, standing on the plush carpet under the recessed lighting, the faint noise of that air made inside seem even nicer than it already was.

"What would you like to hear?" he asked us. "You'll like this," he said and he put on a record we didn't have at home that sounded like the kind of stuff on the radio we'd hear when Dad looked for new music. Dad'd spend about a week trying out the radio and then get fed up and put on his old records.

"Where in the salt-blasted earth did you hear that fucking lie?" Aunt Gabie yelled from the kitchen and then there was a noise like the laundry falling onto the floor. This stopped Miller right in the middle of his explanation of the older bottle caps he had. "Is everyone all right?"

He looked at us. He got up.

Gabie came into the living room and grabbed her coat.

"What's going on?"

"I'm taking Amy to the hospital. I think her arm's broke."

"Is she okay?"

"Her arm's broke. Do you think she's okay?"

Aunt Gabie didn't look at us. She checked her coat for her keys and put on her glasses and looked at herself in the mirror.

"What happened?"

"I'll be back," Aunt Gabie said. "Make some hot chocolate for the boys." Then she left with Amy.

The car lights shone through the front window. Gravel sounded under the car. When it left the darkness returned. The wind hissed against the walls of the house.

Miller stood by the front door.

"I wonder what that was about."

We didn't say anything.

"You get along with Amy?"

"Yeah."

"What did you talk about when you went bike riding?"

"About her adjusting to being out here," I said. I looked at my brother who I could see wanted to say something. Damon pinched his bottom lip with his upper teeth. We sat on the couch and stared at Miller's bottle cap collection. Miller nodded his head and went into the kitchen.

"Why aren't you telling him?" my brother asked me.

"He doesn't want to know," I said. "You shouldn't say anything."

He came back with the hot chocolate and handed it to us. "Here you go," he said.

"Thanks," my brother said. "Maybe Aunt Gabie is upset because of what my brother said while we were bicycling."

"Yes?" Miller asked. He set his beer can on the table.

I just sat still because I could on one hand believe that Damon would tell Miller, but on the other hand I had asked him not to tell him and now he was going to go ahead and like a little kid do just what he thought he was supposed to do even if he had been told different. "He asked her if she missed her brother and she was confused because she didn't know she had a brother and so he told her about her brother."

"What brother?"

"You don't know about Aunt Gabie's other baby?"

"Oh, her *other* baby," he said. "The one that isn't my child."

"I don't know," Damon said.

While we drank the hot chocolate, we listened to the rest of the record. Miller went back to the kitchen and came back with a can of Olympia Beer. "You can pick a record," Miller said. We paged through his records looking for one that we recognized but we couldn't tell what they sounded like or what they might be and so finally we picked a record with a glowing flying saucer on the cover. "This one?" my brother said.

"A Boston fan amongst us?" Miller nodded. He put it on the turntable and when it played, it was just like the first record he'd put on the turntable.

When the songs ended, we could hear the wind blowing dust against the side of the home. Finally, the car light shone against the side of the house. Aunt Gabie and Amy came in. Amy had a balloon and a sling.

"What are they still doing up?" she asked Miller.

"You didn't tell me what to do with them."

Amy went to her room. Her balloon bounced on the ceiling behind her.

"Time for bed boys," Aunt Gabie said.

In addition to his fear of rattlesnakes, millipedes, and ghosts, my brother was afraid of the dark. After we brushed our teeth and washed our faces, we climbed into bed in the spare bedroom where Aunt Gabie had laid out two foam mattresses fitted with sheets and blankets. "Good night boys," Aunt Gabie said. When she turned out the light there was no light in the house or outside. It was very, very black and quiet except for the constant scratching of the wind. We could hear, though, the faint voices rising and falling of Miller and Aunt Gabie in their bedroom. Trying to hear what they were saying, I finally fell asleep. And then I woke up. My brother had brushed his hand against my face. "I need to go to the bathroom," he said.

"You know where it is," I said.

"I know," he said.

We waited for a long time listening in the house. There was just the sound of the wind now. Aunt Gabie and Miller had stopped talking. Just as I started to fall back asleep, my brother said, "Please?"

"No," I said because to be honest, I didn't want to leave our room either.

He got up. "I can't see."

He fumbled around until he finally opened the door. I fell back asleep.

Aunt Gabie found him in the morning. He had crawled into the hallway and then, terrified, he froze. After waiting for how long—hours?—he defecated. He had defecated there in the dark because he could no longer hold it. At eight years old, he was potty trained and he had been for some time. He had crawled out there and then became so scared he couldn't move.

She yelled at him. "What is going on here?" She made him clean up the mess and her yelling woke the rest of the house and we all came out, all of us trying to stand in the narrow little hallway with my brother on his hands and knees scrubbing with a bucket of warm soapy water.

"Why did you do that?" my Aunt Gabie asked over and over again.

"I was scared," my brother cried.

"You have no respect for my house."

"It was an accident."

"It can only be done on purpose."

"I didn't mean to do it."

"You might have subconsciously meant to do it," she said. "But you meant to do it. It was done in my hall."

Once we were dressed, my aunt drove us back to my grandmother's house in Ephrata. My aunt didn't get out of the car. She didn't take off her sunglasses and instead of her eyes we could only see the truck dashboard, our own faces looking back at her, and then the road and prairie. Everything was flat and warped in the reflection. Grandma had a root beer bottle in her hand and a lit cigarette in the other. She put the cigarette in her mouth to free a hand to wave good-bye to Aunt Gabie. She handed the root beer to me. "You can come in when you feel like it," she said. "We'll play poker later."

It was my turn to open the bottle of root beer, but I handed it to my brother. "Go ahead," I said. "Open it."

"No," he said. "I'll open it and you'll think everything is all right again." He placed the shiny bottle on the porch rail. The screen snapped behind him. I wasn't going to open that bottle now. Later in the middle of betting, Grandma just came out and asked me. "Why didn't you help your brother?" And I knew he'd told her what happened or probably Aunt Gabie had said something and she'd figured out what had happened.

"I didn't know he needed my help," I said. "I was asleep."

I waited for Damon to say something because he knew I wasn't telling it completely like it was. Later Damon sat on the porch listening to the sprinklers and the crickets. I thought, he might be trying to hear a rattlesnake, still. He didn't say anything.

# Super Sport

DAD'S SUPER SPORT IMPALA CONVERTIBLE, a large car already, seems much larger now that Mom is driving away from him. The beater doesn't exactly have a great running record, so it sort of seemed weird to me that Mom chose this as her getaway car. Blair, he's my older brother, asks Mom, "Who's going to fix the Impala when something stops working?" At this point we've been driving for a long time, maybe an hour, and I think both Blair and I had it in the back of our heads that Mom is just driving to show off, to make a point, and that as soon as she gets to Wenatchee she'll turn around. Mom doesn't even stop for the red light in Wenatchee.

"We can always find a mechanic dying to help me," Mom says. "I take one look at the way I lived with your father, at his house with his dear old fruit trees that don't bare fruit; the mossy roof that doesn't keep out the rain; the three rusted out Chevies on blocks in the pasture that don't run; I realize I'm not that kind of person."

Blair, he's my older brother, calls her on that right away. "But

Grey and I are those kinds of people. We grew up with those cars in the pasture."

"You're not grown yet." Mom reaches over to pat Blair on his head. He ducks and checks his hair in the rearview mirror. "Your father," Mom says, "is that kind of people. We aren't. We care about one another and like to read books and sing even though we're pretty bad at it, don't we?"

I cover my ears and say, "That's not a cue to sing 'California Dreaming,'" to get us out of this line of questioning. Blair can go off the handle if he thinks someone is putting him down.

Mom launches her off-key warble. Blair rolls his eyes and I smile but after about two minutes I wish Mom would calm down. She keeps going because she knows after another minute or so we'll join in just because if we're making all that noise, too, we'll enjoy it some. Anything, up and to and including singing along with Mama Cass Elliot, is better than listening to my mother singing alone to Mama Cass Elliot.

I don't really understand what Mom means about her not being that kind of person. Everyone is like everyone else, as far as I can tell, so all of this talk about kinds of people doesn't really mean much to me. Given a choice, everyone is going to want donuts and hamburgers.

I do know it's cool to be in Dad's car without him. Blair sits in the front seat with Mom, and they play music on the radio Dad would never let us play. I have the entire back seat to myself. I spread out, stretching my legs from one end to the other of the long bench. Blair rolls the dial until he finds the song he's stuck on. It's John Cougar Mellencamp's song called "Jack and Diane." I can tell Mom already hates it, even if she plays along like everything we're doing right now is great. Instead of screaming or turning the radio off or doing anything we would expect her to do, she sings along with the song.

"Cut it out, Mom," Blair says.

He starts to get pissed because Mom makes it sound really goofy. *This is a little ditty about Jack and Diane*, the song goes, but Mom throws in this uh-huh in a deep voice between "Jack" and "Diane." *This is a little ditty about Jack uh-huh Diane.*

"Mom, I'm serious. That's not cool."

Mom keeps it up until Blair snaps the radio off.

"Kids," Mom says in her deep voice, like she's planning on doing something and I wish she would because when Blair gets like this, no one can tell what he's going to do. He folds the sports section over his face and lays back in the bucket seat. The wind jumping around the convertible keeps the paper plastered to his face. I just sit on my hands, waiting until we get wherever we're going. I think about Dad in Grandma's house, where Mom left him sitting at the kitchen table. He didn't even come outside when we left. He'd been busy rolling a joint and tapping his foot to an old harmonica blues song playing on his portable tape player.

Blair was the first to run away. We didn't know where he'd gone. Dad said, "Well, the boy is grown. He'll get in touch with us once he gains his feet. Kids always do. He'll need money for a deposit or something." When Blair finally came back from wherever he was, Dad was angry. "Why in the hell are you leaving if you aren't ready? This ain't a flophouse. You think your mother and I didn't have to work to get where we are? To get this house? To get this car?" When Blair come back it was almost like he'd left something behind only he didn't know what it was. He was always trying to see if I could figure it out. "Things used to be so cool," he said. "And now they suck." I thought when Mom packed Blair and me in the car at Grandma's it was in order to find whatever it was that Blair had lost. When Blair and I were really little we once went swimming in the gravely North Fork of the Snoqualmie River, way up the rapids, along the old logging roads, over the rickety trestle bridges. Out of the smooth, heavy river stones I built a castle in the middle of the shallow stream. In the middle of the castle, I had an enclosed lake. I floated my wooden toy blocks in the still water and admired how still they bobbed up and down on the silvery water when all around the thick castle walls the cold river gurgled and hummed as millions of gallons of water just rolled on and on. One of the stones slipped free and all of the blocks glided into the rapids. I felt hot water trickle down my cheeks as I tried to catch up with the blocks in the swiftly running river. I lifted my foot up. I brought it down into deep current. I tried to stand on the rocks. The blocks spread out over the entire river. On the slippery stones, I could barely stand half a step from my castle. I dove for a bright yellow triangle and plunged into the knee-deep snowmelt, stood, and slipped again. The entire time the blocks raced away. I know big things have happened to me since, but whenever Dad would take Blair and me up the North Fork Road, I'd think about those blocks slipping away. I'd had them for as long as I could remember up until they just floated away, down the rapids, probably getting stuck in a mossy bank where their bright yellow, red, or blue paint would fade. I sort of thought Blair felt like that now, and he was angry because he didn't know who'd taken this thing away from him. He thought maybe Dad had taken it, or maybe Mom had taken it away, or even me.

For lunch, we stop at a McDonald's near a big city I'd never been to before. Mom says it's Spokane and that it has the biggest railyards in the entire state of Washington. "Spokane," she says, "was built by hobos who decided this place must be nowhere enough that they never left." We drive through the drive-thru and sit in the parking lot. A lot of people must do that because as soon as we park, we're looking over this huge field covered with rusting railroad tracks, rotting wooden boxcars, grimy warehouses, and trillions of telephone poles sent tiny birds from the electric wires. The birds are so dirty, when they land on the filthy parking lot asphalt they almost look invisible. Flocks of them dive at the car. Sixty-two of them skip across the hood. Their feathers tuff up and the white stuffing from under their wings spins into the air. Dad would have murdered us if we'd touched the turtle-waxed surface with one of our french fry greasy fingers. These birds land on the door sill, cheeping and chirping, and cocking their heads, pretending to be cute, even though they look like living dog turds. They keep coming. One bird gets stuck under the seat and Blair tries to kick it out. He sits up on the side of the car, throwing his french fries. They bounce off bird heads and other birds pluck the fries in mid-air with fifty other birds in hot pursuit. Finally, Blair rolls off the back of the Impala, and reaches past Mom, who must be frozen because the birds are so frigging ugly. Blair pulls the keys out of the ignition. He doesn't seem to mind that he has just left his hamburger on the seat where the birds swarm like huge flies. Four of them rip the burger apart and another takes flight with the yellow wrapper.

Blair throws open the trunk. I think he's going to crawl inside. Instead, he pulls out his yellow whiffle-ball bat and starts beating the sides of the car, something I can't believe even if Dad isn't here. He whacks the front of the hood over and over again and the birds fly up to the telephone wires. Some of them just sort of hover over him as he swings the bat. The whiffle-bat makes its hollow scream and nails a sparrow. The little bird drops onto the hood and rolls onto the pavement.

"Blair," Mom finally says. "They're gone. Come back in the car."

Blair doesn't even hear her. He stamps on the bird even though he's wearing his new tennis shoes. He throws the crushed body at the electric wires and then he starts chucking rocks at them and screaming, "I'm going to kill every one of you!" Mom grabs Blair by his shoulders and he jumps around; his face is pale. Sweat runs from under his hair. His eyes are almost closed. Mom steps back and away from him. I don't know if he's going to hit Mom or what.

At last Mom says, "You go inside that McDonald's and wash your hands. Those birds are covered in germs." She hands him some money to buy a new hamburger.

"You don't know anything about germs." He leans down like he is going to tackle Mom or something and scoops up a handful of gravel and throws it straight up into the sky. The rocks hang high up in the air for a second and then scatter everywhere, bouncing off the car, rattling on the pavement, raining down on Blair and Mom. She grabs Blair by the back of his upper arm and drags him into the McDonald's. As soon as he's halfway across the lot, his shoulders droop, and I feel sort of sorry for him. The birds even stay away until he's gone into the McDonald's, and then they flock down from the wires, out of the shadows of the railyard, and cover the car.

Mom zips past cars on the highway. On the upside of the hills, she signals and swerves the convertible into the far lane next to the double yellow line. The warm air rushes over the car, rushing into the backseat. My ears ring. On one hill, we pass a slow moving dump truck filled with junked cars. In the Eastern Washington weather, under the heavy snow, under the bright summer heat, the chrome has rusted as brittle and brown as bacon strips.

Eastern Washington, the other half of the state, is dry, hot, and land locked. Visiting grandma, I often thought of her house as the place where I could see the clouds in the sky. The sky is large here. The surface of the prairie rolls on and on like rocky ocean swells. Western Washington, where I am from, is damp, cold, and never more than an hour from sea water. Puget Sound isn't the open ocean, but I can still find tidal pools with starfish, kelp, and seaweed with woody floater knots. All day long, Mom drives across Eastern Washington on the highway. I don't know where she is going. Maybe she is running away but it seems unlikely she is going to get anywhere if she's dragging Blaire and me along. The dry wind whips across my face, and I drink soda, and I drink the water I put in the soda bottle but I am still thirsty. Just looking at the crooked fence posts and the sagebrush makes my mouth dry. Parched grass and empty gulches roll on and on until even a single dead tree is a relief.

Mom guns the Impala past the dump truck. The man driving it, his half-bald head surrounded by unwashed strands of stray hair, wears aviator sunglasses. He touches the tip of his index finger to the rim of the glasses and honks his horn. He wears a black T-shirt discolored by bleach stains. The exhaust pipe rising up behind the cab spills black smoke. The truck, with its wide tires and loaded body, strains up the grade.

Mom doesn't even turn around to wave at the driver. She waves at him through the rearview mirror brushing the surface of the mirror with the tips of her fingers like she's cleaning it. Mom wears a white dress and a light blue cardigan and her hair is tied behind her head with a piece of blue ribbon. It occurs to me then how she must see herself, a young blond in a convertible. It's just that Blair and I sit there to total her image.

The Super Sport's speedometer ends at 120 miles an hour, and the needle flaps against 80. "Faster, Mom," Blair says. "Faster. Take off right off this hill." We sail over the top, and although the car doesn't lose contact with the asphalt, the seat belt is the only thing that keeps me on my seat. We sail down the hill. Blair howls and Mom turns back over to the slow lane because on this side of the hill the oncoming traffic has the extra lane. The engine made a gurgling sound and popped. Something is wrong with the car, then. We can feel it because instead of accelerating down the hill, the Impala begins to make a faint noise. We don't slow down to fifty until we start to climb the next hill. We climb the hill at forty miles and hour. The car pops again and we pick up speed. We go down the next hill at forty miles an hour and finally the dump truck comes up to our bumper. This time, though, the man lays on his horn until Mom pulls the car over to the shoulder. Dust sprays up and fills the inside of the convertible with grains of sand. He doesn't even look at us as he eases the truck over the double yellow line. I can't see his eyes past his sunglasses; instead I see pillowy clouds moving along the Eastern Washington sky.

When the car slows down, it doesn't regain its speed. Mom has the pedal all of the way to the floorboard and the car can barely go twenty-miles an hour. Mom guns the car, and it doesn't do anything. It just revs up, and then idles down and that's it.

"What's wrong?" Blair asks. The radio starts to cut out, and then it goes dead. "Damn it."

"The car is broken," Mom says.

"I am not a moron," Blair says. "I can tell it ain't working."

"Ain't, ain't a word," Mom says.

"Stop the car. I'll fix it."

"You can have a look, I guess. You won't leave it in worse shape than it is." She turns to see if any traffic is coming. A Ford pickup clears the top of the hill, now way behind us, and we are already climbing another hill. The red Ford starts to slow down and Blair jumps up and shakes his head. The driver waves and keeps driving on its way.

"Why did you do that?" Mom asks.

"We don't need any guy like that interfering."

"He could have given us a lift to the next town. We are going to need a mechanic."

"I can fix it," Blair says. He opens the hood of the car. The engine smells like gasoline and singed oil. A faint blue smoke hangs over the engine. Blair touches the hose coming out of the radiator. "Fuck." He looks back to see if Mom heard him. She just rolls her eyes and watches the highway. Blair swaggers back to the trunk and takes out the whiffle ball bat, the suitcase, and finally finds Dad's black toolbox.

"We had those in there?"

"Yep," Blair says. He takes the tools out of the case, lays out a cloth, and then lays out wrenches and screwdriver and clamps, examining each one as he does this. After he has all the tools laid out and displayed, he nods and then begins removing pipes, and filters. He did something to a pipe. Finally, he put everything back together. Mom and I wait in the car, looking sort of scared at each other each time a car passes. Without even trying the car, Blair puts each tool away as precisely as he took them out. He scoots Mom over with a flick of his hand and sits down in her seat. He tries the engine and it fires and starts, kicking out clouds of blue smoke. "See," Blair says. Another car, a station wagon, passes us, slows down and stops. "Get in the car," Blair tells Mom.

"I'm driving," she says.

"Yeah, yeah," Blair says, but he steps on the gas and Mom has to throw herself in the bucket seat or she's going to be left behind. The man by this time smiles and walks back toward us. His family sits in the car. They all have their Sunday clothes on. He wears a gray suit and black, shiny shoes. The man leans against the station wagon and Mom barely gets her door closed, or the door would have winged the man. Blair swerves out into the oncoming lanes and we are on our way. "See, the car is fixed. Dad wasn't good for nothing. He could always get this heap moving."

"Blair, I should drive."

"Let me drive to the next town."

"You just about ran that poor man down. He was trying to help us."

"He was interfering. We didn't need help. You may need help. But I don't."

Mom doesn't say anything. She keeps glancing behind her, but there isn't a car or anything. Blair drives with one hand on the steering wheel and changes the dial to find his song. When he finds what he is looking for, he nods his head in time to the beat and spreads his arm out over the back of Mom's seat.

We pass a crossroads with a dented sign that points toward Moscow and another toward Missoula. "Go to Moscow," Mom says. "They'll have a mechanic."

Blair turns toward Missoula. He accelerates and the car groans a long rising noise like a soda bottle that has been shaken. The car pops again. And then the actual animation of the car, whatever force kept all of that steel and iron and chrome and vinyl going had just kept going and left the steel and iron and the chrome and vinyl and us behind. "What the fucking damn shit hell," Blair says. Blair slows the car down and barely gets it off the road. There aren't any ditches here. The sides of the road fall all of the way down to the field. Rows of corn go on and on all of the way to the top of the next hill. Along the ridge of the hill, the irrigation tractors rise up like giant picket fences. The car comes to rest on the access road. Blair slams the horn down. He jumps outside and hollers, "Fuck!"

"Blair," Mom says. "Please stop using that language."

"You said those words don't mean shit. Fuck is just a fucking blank fucking space."

"They're nonsense syllables, but if you said 'apple pie' the way you say 'fuck' or 'piss', I wouldn't want you to use them either. People will identify what kind of person you are by the kind of language you use. They have nothing else to go on besides the way you look. And Blair honey, there isn't anything you can do about that, blessed with your father's look and all. But you can speak pleasantly."

"Screw you too, Mom."

"See? What kind of person do I think you are?"

"You've thought I was an asshole from the day I was born."

"You were a sweet baby. You're still kind of cute when you don't use that urinal of a mouth. All you can do to let people know what kind of person you are is talk. Talk like the kind of person you want to be, and you will be that person."

"What? If you were my mother, then where's my Dad? Why do you always have to leave someone behind?"

"It's very constructive of you to point out my mistakes." Mom doesn't even look at Blair. She stares through her reflection in the windshield. "Though you don't appreciate it, I'm very aware that my mistakes hurt you. But just because I'm your mother, that doesn't mean I'm the enemy."

"Too fucking late," Blair says. He jumps out of the car.

"Blair, will you stop using that filth. Blair, fix this," she says. She opens the trunk and tosses the black case at Blair. He catches it. Mom doesn't even look at him. She takes the bag of groceries and the blanket out of the trunk. We go out and sit on the knoll above the irrigation ditch. We don't even listen to Blair cursing and making all of that noise. After we eat our lunch, Mom and I walk through the corn. We walk all of the way up to the row of irrigation tractors. At the top of that hill, we can see the same kinds of hills all around us. There is the highway going through this space, and all of those hills going on and on for as far as we can see, well, until the sky starts. A row of poplar trees grows just beyond the horizon. "That's a farm house," Mom says.

"How can you tell?" I asked.

"Wind break," she says. At the car she asks Blair, "You fix that thing, yet?"

"Just about," Blair says.

"What do you think is wrong with it?"

"This and that," he says.

"Grey and I are going over to that farm house," Mom says. "We're going to get us a ride into Moscow. You want to come with us or stay here? We will be back."

"Can I have the keys. Because if I don't have the keys... I won't be able to tell if I fixed the car or not."

"I'm not giving you the keys."

"If you don't give me the keys, I'll be forced to hot wire it."

"Well, if that's how it is," Mom says.

"If I have to hot wire it, I won't be here when you get back."

"It's not your car," Mom says.

"It's not your car, either. I figure, if it's stolen already, then it's fair game, ain't it?"

"Ain't ain't a word," Mom says.

Blair shouts at us as we walk up the access road toward those poplars, "When I hot wire this car, I'll be long gone by the time you get back."

David wears a blue shirt over a white T-shirt with the letters DAVID stitched into his pocket. A spiral notepad sticks out of his pocket. A fountain pen pinches the side of his pocket. "I like your pen," Mom says as he writes down the information about our car. His hair is very short, even shorter than that of the pheasant hunters who used to camp in the woods behind our house. He wrinkles his eyes and they disappear under the flaps of skin over his brown eyes. "Thank you very much," he says. "My mother always had a thing for writing instruments. She hated typewriters. She wouldn't even use one when she worked as a secretary in an insurance office. You can imagine that didn't go over too well. She was big on the human touch."

He squirts a shot of greenish soap like a teaspoon of apple mint jelly onto his hands and rubs his palms together until he holds a ball of bubbles. Layers of ancient motor oil and unknown gunk coat the sink basin. When David rinses, his hands are callused and clean except for black crescents lodged into the rims of his fingernails. My father's hand had the same red burnished calluses and always smelled like engine oil, a bitter buttery odor.

"Walt," David says, "I'm going to go get these folks' car."

Walt peeks out from behind the hood of a truck and muttered something and then went back to work. A radio faintly plays. David drives a red tow truck that smells like plastic and coffee. Every time David racks the gearshift, I jump. Before we get out there, Mom warns David about Blair. "I have a sixteen year old son. He's trying to fix the car."

"Maybe it'll be fixed."

"He said he'd hot wire it and take off if I didn't wait for him."

"We can always hope," David says, but quickly apologizes when we don't laugh. "Sixteen years old is rough. Nobody escapes without doing something radically stupid."

Before we get to the access road we find Blair walking in the middle of the road. He doesn't even clear out of the way. "That's him," Mom says. David stops the truck directly in front of him.

Blair shields his eyes as he looks into the car. He jumps at the hood. David throws open the door and leans out to pull Blair down. As soon as Blair sees David, he starts to run. Blair jumps off the highway, the irrigation water and weeds rushing down the ditch. He runs. David keeps after him, though, and brings Blair down into the dusty field with a very professional looking tackle. He wraps Blair in some wrestling maneuver. Blair doesn't even have his feet on the ground. Finally, Blair shouts something, and David sinks into the knee-deep dirt. David and Blair shake hands, and they walk back to the truck.

"Thank you, David," Mom says.

"No problem, ma'am."

"Linda," Mom says.

"Pleased to meet you, Linda."

"Now, shall we get the car?" Mom asks Blair.

"I kind of hot wired it," Blair says. "And then drove it into the ditch. It's about a half-mile up the road." Where Blair had been sitting erect in the seat and glancing over the crown of our heads, he now huddled in his space in the cab of the tow truck.

"This is the greatest car America ever built," Walt says. He wears blue and white pin striped overalls, with big brass buttons. Oil blackens his long, gray beard.

"America?" Mom says in a loud voice. "Don't that mean the world?" Blair smiles at me because we know Mom is making fun of the guy, but he had to notice that it sounds like something he'd say himself. Walt laughs out loud when Mom says that, "Damn right. We'll have your car fixed up by tomorrow." He looks at David. "We have to get a new radiator driven in from Spokane."

"Thanks," Mom says.

Blair picks up a tool and Walter grabs his wrist. "Keep your paws in your pockets."

"Mom," I say, "we don't have any money."

"We have enough. Besides, people don't always want money."

The cinderblock motel we finally decide to stay at doesn't have a swimming pool. It does have a Coke machine, a new one with Sprite and Coke and Welch Grape. Our room looks out over a field of young green corn, hardly up to my knees. Pools of standing water lay close to the motel. Algae coats the pools like organic oil slicks. Blair and I set out a row of cans at the edge of the field and throw the largest rocks we can find at them. They are about the size of grammar school marbles with just enough heft to actually throw the distance we want. They aren't even heavy enough to knock the cans into the ponds. They glance off the stones and disappear into the water, breaking the algae for a second, and then the skin closes up. At last, I nail a can— bullseye—and it falls into the pond and floats there getting its sides covered with whatever that stuff is.

Mom leaves with David as soon as she drops us off at the motel. On the way over, she stops by the town grocer and bought two TV dinners and a carton of Neapolitan ice cream, so it isn't much of a surprise to Blair and me when she says she was going to go out with David for a drink. Blair calls her on it anyway.

"You mean you're just having a drink and you'll be back for supper?"

"Honey, I only bought two TV dinners. You got that far in school. You do the arithmetic." She scoops Blair's face in her hand. Her nails close over his eyes like a cage, and she gives him a big, fresh lipstick smack on the lips.

Blair just stares at the grocery bag she leaves on the table. He doesn't even wipe off the make-up or anything. He looks at me. "If she is going to go out with a man like Dad, why can't it just be Dad? That would be a whole lot easier for everyone."

For a while after Mom leaves, Blair is sort of nice. I can tell something is coming though. We go outside and throw those rocks and then finally, we go back inside. It is just Blair and me. He's being real careful not to piss me off, so we have a good time because we don't know if Mom is even going to come back or not. But Blair asks me after we eat the dinners and eat two bowls of ice cream each, "How much money do you got?"

"I haven't had allowance in over four weeks," I say. "I keep asking for a raise—but you know how it is."

"Yeah," Blair says. "I haven't even had an allowance since I got back. I sure miss my allowance. I could buy all of the candy and video games and comic books I wanted. I sure felt like a great little bratty kid blowing my allowance on crap like that. *Boo* fucking *hoo* I sure miss my damn five dollars. It sure was great of those chumps to pay me five big ones for doing nothing except being a kid."

The next morning, we walk across town to the coffee shop next to the garage. It has started to rain even though streaks of sunlight fall over the prairie. The puddles reflect the cloudy sky. Blair and I stand looking at those puddles while we wait outside the cafe. After a long, long time Blair goes into the cafe and then comes outside. "She's gone." He just says it and then we sit there, thinking maybe she has gone away with David and we won't see her again. I start to get mad then because if she did leave like that, then she should have left us with Dad.

Just as we are getting ready to go to the highway to hitchhike or something, a sparkling blue Chevy Malibu pulls up, its engine puttering and blowing out a faint purple vapor. Mom staggers out of the car. Her hair is damp and pulled back into a single ponytail. "Thanks for the ride David," she says.

"No problem-o," David says. He doesn't even look at Blair or me. He just drives out to the end of the parking lot, signals left, and takes a right turn.

Blair stands up into Mom's face, on the balls of his Keds. "Where've you been?"

"It's none of your business, all right, kid," Mom says. That really pisses Blair off. He steps back then and I'm afraid he'll go right off and hit Mom or something so I jump up and run around, "Mom's back in town," I sing. "Let's get in the car and get going."

"I'm not going anywhere with her, now," Blair says. "She's a whore."

"Watch your fucking language," Mom says.

"Fuck ain't a fucking word."

Mom slaps Blair. He slaps her back, right across the face, and we all stop moving then. It doesn't hurt Mom any, but you can tell it wasn't that it hurt so much as the fact that Blair has hit her. Not even Dad has done that before. Blair starts saying how sorry he is for having to hit her, but she hit him first. "Where'd you go? How were we supposed to know you'd come back?"

Mom won't listen to him. He sits in the back seat once we get the car back. Mom and I play old songs on the radio, the songs I like because Mom knows the words to them. She won't sing to them, though. I had thought when Mom packed Blair and me in the car at Grandma's it was in order to find whatever it was that Blair had lost, but really I guess, it was to lose whatever she had found living with Dad, but the only problem was that since she was out she was bound to find something. She'd probably just find the same thing again. I think Blair knows that and that was why he came back, because at least at home he had us. Blair just sits back there, not sleeping or saying anything, even though he hates the music and I'm pretty sure, then, that he hates Mom, and probably hates me.

# Snoqualmie

BRET FIRST SAW THE FIGURE on the railroad tracks during the four-mile walk from his job in North Bend to his apartment in Snoqualmie. He had just finished his dishwashing shift at the Mexican restaurant where he'd started working after he quit the gas station. When he started to walk, the light fell against the top of the upper boughs of the Douglas fir. He walked in the middle of the tracks without thinking about the trains, because the few engines that did run along the tracks inched along and sounded their horn at every curve and trestle. In the dusky summer heat, the creosote drooled and released a resinous vapor that hung in sticky clouds. Two miles further down, the rails passed over the Snoqualmie River, a stretch of deep, green water that hardly showed its sluggish flow. As the light tipped off the top boughs, he saw the figure that he thought might be Martha but couldn't be Martha. She lay buried in the Mount Si cemetery next to her father who had died back in the seventies while felling timber along Quartz Creek.

The figure wore a red and green Mount Si High lettermen's jacket. Bret thought that it was a high school kid, until he noticed that the jacket hung funny. It was too large. He started walking quickly to catch her. He stumbled on the tracks, kicking stones down the steep banks. The figure glanced back at him. He unmistakably saw her long nose and slightly cleft chin. Bret was certain then, because he could see the golden thread spelling out the name SKYLAR, and he knew it was Russ Skylar's coat. Martha was the only person who would still wear it, even if she was lying dead and buried in Mount Si cemetery. She moved briskly down the tracks. The ties were difficult to travel over because they lay at the wrong width for Bret's pace. He tried to ignore the surface, but in the failing light he almost twisted his ankle. He wanted to call her name. But, he wasn't sure if Martha, who had been a year older in school, even remembered who he was.

She finally disappeared around the curve of the tracks. He wasn't sure if he had lost her. At length, he came out to the dirt trail. He found fresh footprints and skids in the mud. He hurried out onto the residential road under the telephone poles next to the newish ramblers with their beds of beauty bark and rhododendrons. He looked up and down the street for her. He passed the junkyard. A man wearing grease-stained overalls worked on the engine of an old Ford truck. A rubber band was wrapped around his beard, and he had tucked the beard length into his shirt. Although Bret often passed the battered tin fence, he rarely saw anyone in the yard. "Hey, have you seen anyone in a lettermen's jacket pass this way?" The hair of the junkman's mustache pulled tight over his lips. His distended belly hung over his thin legs. Several metallic pins clung to the lapel of his overalls, the Standard Oil Pegasus, an enamel classic Rolls Royce, and a tarnished metal disc.

The junkman looked up from the engine. He had dark brown eyes with massive pupils that swallowed the light. He stared at Bret. At last, he blinked. He coughed and leaned behind the truck. He kept his forefinger lifted, and before long, surfaced from the other side of the truck and wheezed. He said something unintelligible through his mustache. A thin stream of blue smoke poured from his mouth. "No, man, nothing." Bret wondered if he had imagined this girl who was supposed to be dead. However, he saw she had left physical evidence, gouges in the muddy bank, a full, flat impression of the foot of her tennis shoe, smaller than his own foot.

Bret lived in a studio apartment at the top of a brick building that stood at the edge of the corn field growing along the river bank. The Snoqualmie River often jumped its bank with the spring snow melt and flooded the entire valley. Three feet of water filled the basement during the flood, driving the mice up onto the first and second floors. If the flood lasted long enough, the rodents infested his cupboards. Up on the hills, all around Snoqualmie, Seattle developers were building new houses. The knock of hammers on two-by-fours and the groan of bulldozers clearing the second growth timber came along with the wind. No one ever bothered the old buildings and dairy fields and corn fields along the flooding river. There had been talk that the developers might buy the houses in the flood plain and tear everything down to make a big park. No one was doing anything like that.

On most days, Bret ate leftover rice and beans from the restaurant. He wore the clothes his parents had bought him, keeping his blue jeans washed, his white shirts bleached, his oxfords polished. He had been a tall boy waiting to grow into his hands and feet and shoulders, but instead of getting larger after his parents died, he'd lost weight until the clothes his mother had bought him were washed ragged and hung in loose folds. Using a hammer and nail, he pounded new holes along the length of his belt. He had told his grandparents he could take care of himself, and as if to demonstrate, he had opened his closet and showed his grandmother his week's clothes already hung on hangers waiting for him. Bret endured a life of waiting, for what he wasn't sure; he didn't expect anything.

Miss Eaves, the manager of Bret's building, often stood among the shoulder-high cornstalks, feeding the flocks of seagulls that shuttled down to eat the flax in the field. Although she pointed out the crows standing on the telephone poles, the shattered roofs of abandoned barns, the pyramid-roofed hop houses, the locations of feral blueberry patches, Bret didn't think of her in the same way he did the old men who smoked pipes on the picnic bench outside the Post Office. To Bret, these old men represented the old citizens of the valley. They'd worked for Weyerhaeuser or Burlington Northern. They recalled bitter, past winters with nostalgia and often debated about the location of buildings and roads that had vanished long ago. Miss Eaves knew where things were right at the present moment in the valley and didn't seem to care much for the ways things used to be.

When Bret moved into the building after his parents died, Miss Eaves spoke with his grandparents. His grandfather wore an old leather bomber jacket even though he had only worked in the kitchen of a carrier in the South Pacific. His grandmother wore a black skirt and matching blouse. She had only packed black clothes and had been wearing black since they had arrived for the funeral. As his grandparents stood in the small studio apartment, grimly staring at the pasture, Miss Eaves grabbed Bret's elbow. They stood in the narrow stairway leading up from the wide, musty third story hallway. "You won't believe it, since to you I'm sure I appear the same age as those two fossils, but I can still dance." She swayed her hips and executed a dance maneuver, tricky in its shifting of feet and accented by her swinging arms. Bret had no idea where the dance came from or why she was showing him this. While she danced, she kept her head turned to one side and her eye on him. She shrugged when she didn't get a response. "You'll have fun here. Move in." Her face fell back into a business-like scowl and she walked back up the stairs to where his grandparents had the cupboards open and were looking inside. "What are these black balls?"

"Mouse droppings," she said. Miss Eaves told Bret's grandparents, "This is very close to the school. The building is occupied by older, sedentary people like myself. Most of us are asleep by nine o'clock and awake by five. You can be assured your boy will have an environment that is both comfortable and wholesome. No need to worry about him throwing parties until all hours of the night. That simply won't be an option at a building like this. I, myself, will look after him as if he were my own grandson. I think it's smart for him to finish school in the same place he started. After all he has been through, no sense in compounding the injury."

His grandparents signed the lease. They sat in the room for a long while with him. They didn't say much except for a few comments on the view of the junkyard, the river, the mountain. "I guess that junkyard makes for a depressing view. At least you can see the river. And the mountain is an eyeful. You'll be happy here." They left him there, alone, with his fruit crates of belongings sitting on the sidewalk. His parents' things had either been sold or had been packed in the U-Haul trailer his grandparents took back to Spokane. Bret carried his things through the lobby, past the Ming vase manufactured in San Diego and the jade artifacts that filled a curio cabinet. A red sofa with a greenish blanket draped over the back sat in front of an empty fireplace. Faded wooden panels lined the hallway walls. The fuzzy balls of moth nests clung to the corners of the ceilings.

"You wouldn't believe it," Miss Eaves said, "but this place used to be quite the party joint in its hey-day, many, many years gone now. When Lester Young played on Jackson in Seattle,

I had enough pull that he stayed a week. This place has seen better days, sure, but it just needs the right set of people to get it hopping again."

"Who's Lester Young?"

She started to roll her eyes and then shook her head. "Check his records out from the library." Miss Eaves wore a long white dress and a knitted shawl with long fringes. Her face was lined with wrinkles, but her pale white arms were as firm and buttery white as baby corn except for the flecks of a few dark brown moles. She lifted the shawl up and flung it around her shoulders. She turned around on the stairway. "Get a life, kiddo."

The next time he saw Miss Eaves, she wore a heavy, quilted coat. Her coarse gray hair twisted with dark brown hung down over her face. Dark creases cut into the skin around her mouth. She stopped and blinked at him and cowered in the corner of the lobby. A janitorial bucket full of ammonia sat in the middle of the tile floor. Pine needles and hair lay in a scummy ring around the edge of the pungent fluid. Instead of saying anything, she lifted her black rubber gloved hands to make an inarticulate gesture. She set herself down on her knees and continued to scrub, with a lethargic shift of her hips. Bret wanted to help her, but he also didn't want to get roped into cleaning the place up on a regular basis, so he just rushed back up the stairs. In his room, he could hear the bucket rattle.

After this, he occasionally saw Miss Eaves in odd places, perched on a snag in the middle of the Snoqualmie River, or while hiking he saw her standing in the center of a remote clearing in the second-growth forest. She waved. Bret kept going, resisting the impulse to see what she was doing, alone, swaying among the foxglove and daisies. He waved back and kept on his way. he had very little to do with Miss Eaves, except when the flood warnings came and all of the tenants moved everything out of the basement.

However, the morning after he'd seen Martha, Miss Eaves woke him by slamming on his door until he thought the apartment building had been caught in a flash flood. The light came through the old, thick uneven glass panes on the eastern wall. "Do you see them?" she asked. "They're watching us from the junkyard." Bret couldn't see anything, but he thought maybe he was missing something. Stacks of engine blocks, long corrugated tin fences, a rusted school bus cast sharp shadows in the early morning light. Light glanced off crushed glass and burnished chrome. She wore a slip and in the orange morning light it was just about as transparent as saran wrap. She had the body of a young woman and the head of an old woman. Bret couldn't help but stare and wonder if all old women, even the stout old widow down the hall, hid bodies like hers. Miss Eaves' face had soft, deep wrinkles, but the skin around her neck, which on so many old people is as loose as an old sock, was smooth and pale and tight. She had small breasts that didn't hang. The old widow at the end of the hallway, who had a lank black cat that she gave a single can of cat food every day, had breasts that hung like long dangling kielbasas under a wash cloth.

Miss Eaves wasn't thick or bloated like the woman down the hallway, nor was Miss Eaves wiry and stunted like the maintenance man who wore dark green slacks and old motorcycle goggles as he mowed the weeds in the grassy median with his weedwacker. Miss Eaves smelled odd. She shook and he wondered if she was drunk. She smelled like a frayed electrical cord. He didn't know what she could have drank. He put his army surplus overcoat over her shoulders. The long coat trailed on the ground. He walked her downstairs with his arms around her shoulders. He found her apartment door standing open. He put her down into her bed and only remembered his overcoat when he finally lay back down in his own bed. In the morning, he found the coat folded into a neat square at the foot of his door.

He didn't know where to find out about the appearance of old bodies. He finally thought of his friend Jerry's parents, bookish granola-types who had converted every wall of the place into bookshelves, and even though Jerry had left for Seattle long ago, they encouraged Bret to borrow books. When he knocked on the door, Mrs. Frazier answered. She smiled at him and asked him how he was holding up. "Have you made any plans?" Bret said things were coming together, but he wanted to check out their books to find something to read. In their den he finally found evidence of old bodies in a photo book about nude beaches, which not even Jerry had bothered to move into his room because, instead of all kinds of naked bodies frolicking on the beach, armies of naked buxom vixens and such, the photos only showed crowds of old people playing gin rummy, completely nude, old couples strolling through rose gardens, completely nude, happy old people eating Fourth of July spreads of watermelon, hamburgers, hot-dogs, potato salad, completely, utterly nude. He realized that Miss Eaves really did have an extraordinarily supple body, even if she had the dried apple-head of a sixty-five-year-old woman. Clothes themselves were not a matter of modesty, Bret figured. They were a matter of sanity and vanity and beauty because a nice sweater and pair of jeans looked better than a gaping belly button and a scraggly patch of pubic hair.

After seeing Martha on the train tracks, he began to walk with a sense that there were many things just beyond his vision, or in the shadows under the tangles of blackberries, or hiding in the heavy boughs of the cedar trees that he couldn't explain. He was both afraid he would see Martha again and afraid he would never see her again. He thought over what he would say, but he couldn't plan a speech. "You probably don't remember me..." his speech might start. He didn't know. Every night the journey took longer and longer as he grew more and more desperate to see her again. Then, one night, he saw a woman lying on the far side of a field in a pile of bracken fern. Tall spindly flowers filled the clearing. Bret stumbled down the track, and as the stones clacked, the woman sat up and brushed her dark hair out of her eyes. It was Miss Eaves. She wore a pair of blue jeans. Splatters of oil paint covered the front of her thighs. She wore a white T-shirt, a ratty cardigan, and a scarf around her neck. A tarnished silver clasp pulled her hair back. "What are you doing here?" she asked.

"Miss Eaves?"

"Can you do me the favor of carrying my basket home?"

"Were you sleeping?"

"I don't think so," she said. "I was concentrating. I paint pictures."

Her basket lay in the middle of the field. It was full of pale pink and orange salmon berries, mushrooms, and green, curled fiddle heads. A spiral bound notebook, its cover bent and covered with fruit stains, kept a cloth from blowing away. Bret tried to see what she was concentrating on, but he couldn't make out where she was looking, although it was getting dark. A green and red lettermen jacket lay folded near the basket. SKYLAR. She put on the jacket and he realized then it was her jacket, and that she had somehow found it, maybe at the Antique Barn where everyone moving out of town sold their stuff. The forest at the edge of the clearing that had once seemed alive with the possibilities of the dead, a place where Martha and even his parents could have stumbled out and walked down the railroad tracks, became just acres of unkempt trees covered in moss and mold and rotting leaves. The muddy surge of the Snoqualmie River became a mucky and stinking flow of run-off.

"I was very inspired today," Miss Eaves said. She folded up her blanket. She put on her jacket. "You like my new jacket?"

"It's used," Bret said.

"New used, then. It was the only one I saw in good shape."

He carried her basket back down the tracks. But he didn't say anything when she started to talk to him about learning to live in a place. She talked rapidly, a flow of words that backed up into a stutter and then quickly unraveled. She talked about how clear, accurate observation is vital to understanding where you live. "Everyone just flies off and goes looking for something when they aren't going to find it. I suspect a person gets an unsettled feeling. They think if they leave a place they'll come to a new place that doesn't know that unsettled feeling. Way it is, though, trees and rivers and buildings don't know anything about a feeling of disease." She stopped on the side of the tracks and said, "I was looking for these." She leaned down and brushed her hand over a clump of dark brown mushrooms. They had thin, circular hoods like brown pen caps. She pulled them out and tossed them into the basket.

"I suppose you have a girlfriend," she said. "Well, someone?"

"The girl I loved died. But you know how it is, after a while you go on and don't even think about the person much anymore. When you do realize you're thinking about them, you realize that you've been thinking about them all along. I guess you get used to those kinds of thoughts. It makes you wonder how many other things you've got running in your mind all of the time."

His back hurt by the time they arrived at the apartment building. He set her basket inside her door, and she asked him to move it closer to the window.

He wanted to say something, but he didn't know how he could let her know he understood what she was talking about because, really, he didn't understand, but he liked her speaking to him. He didn't want to offend her. He looked around the walls, at little paintings framed on the wall, and larger paintings hanging from wires across the top of the room and even a couple hanging from the ceiling. He realized then that the walls of the entire room were images of other places, places he'd been, he realized, but with things distorted, missing, added, recombined. There were people he recognized from the building. Nothing, he thought, looked as it should.

Martha had died in the drunk-driving accident that had killed Bret's own parents. In recreating the entire scene on a dry board shortly after the accident, the county deputy had told the reporters from *The Valley Recorder* and *The Seattle Times*, "Just sit tight while I draw this out." Bret's father had been a drinker and driving home from a late night party in December, a night with black ice warnings and a heavy fog, his Honda Accord had cut a sharp corner. A restored Ford Mustang cut the oncoming corner going about forty miles an hour faster than the recommended speed of twenty miles an hour. The Mustang slammed into the rear panel of the Accord. Skimming the surface of the ice-glazed road, Bret's father pulled a hard right on the steering wheel. The Accord spiraled into the stand of vine maples and road-crew-mangled cedar on the upper part of the river bank. The Snoqualmie River came down a long stretch of rapids just upriver, and then raced into the deep, soft soil on the valley floor and cut right into the side of the hill. The hillside the road crossed was steep enough that mud slides often washed over the pavement right down into the deep green water. The car broke through the line of sumac, passed over the lip of the levee, and plunged down the slope into the dark river. The county deputy found the Accord a quarter mile down stream. The seat belts had held both of Bret's parents in their places. The Mustang had jumped the road, tumbled up the bank and into a grove of cedar trees. Russ Skylar, also pretty tanked, drove the Mustang.

He survived. The passenger, Martha, died on impact. A month later, Russ drowned himself in the Snoqualmie. He had jumped from the steel girder bridge Bret could see from his apartment window.

At the time of the accident, Russ and Martha had been out of school for a year. Bret remembered running into Russ at the Milk Barn a few weeks before the crash. Bret was on his way to a party one Friday night after a football game. Bret wore his team jersey and picked up a pack of gum and a hot dog. "Hey, Bret," Russ said. Russ wore his old jersey, number three. This number had for years been the one that all of the players wanted because Irvine Saxon, the only pro-ballplayer to have ever gone to Mount Si High School, had been number three. The year Russ had been quarterback Russ had also been number three and then when Bret's friend Jerry was quarterback the next year, they lost their first two games and Jerry changed his number to thirty-three. Russ was the last number three.

"You going over to Jerry's?" Russ asked him.

Bret couldn't figure out why Russ was wasting his time at the Milk Barn when Martha was somewhere waiting for him. Bret wanted to invite Russ over to Jerry's because he wanted to find out why Martha liked him, but no one at Jerry's including Bret liked him; in fact, they all wondered why Russ hadn't gone to Seattle to start a real job or hadn't gone away to school instead of working part-time at the feed store, where he'd worked in the corrugated tin warehouse on the South Fork Road from his fourteenth birthday to the day Russ would kill himself.

"Naw," Bret said. "See you later, man." As Bret drove over to Jerry's house, Russ followed him. He followed him and then, when Bret turned off the highway past the tractor rental place with its rusted combine harvesters and orange backhoes locked up in the yard, Russ turned the lights out on his Toyota truck.

Bret went into the house where all the guys on the football team were sitting around the living room drinking beer out of cans and watching wrestling on Jerry's thirty-six inch. "Russ Skylar is outside."

"Did you invite that loser over to my house?" Jerry asked.

"Naw, man, he followed me here."

Jerry went outside to talk to Russ and came back inside a little while later. "If I catch any of you all here a year after you graduate, I'll personally bust your ass. That sorry fuck doesn't know what to do with himself."

After the accident, Russ had tied his ankles together with one of Martha's braided belts and dropped himself into the cold river. The common diagnosis was that Russ killed himself because he didn't know what else to do with himself. He drank because he was bored. He drove his Mustang at seventy-three miles an hour into a cedar tree because he was drunk. Bret's parents died. Martha died and finally Russ died because of what he'd done. He should have cleared out of town before the winter set in. Growing up there, the kids felt like high school was a waiting room, and going to classes, playing football, drinking, was all part of killing time until they were allowed to be adults. Many of the parents also had the same feeling, that they worked treadmill jobs with the idea that once their kids were out of the house, they could begin the real business of living.

A year after graduation, Bret still lived in his little apartment and told the few people he ran into from high school that he was saving up to go to Bellevue Community College. Mostly, he spent his time in the evening reading the books he'd picked up from the shelves at the Frazier house and his days off hiking or fishing in some creek along the Snoqualmie. He often traveled along a narrow logging road, past the turnaround where the trucks stopped to camp at an overgrown burn pit edged with blackened stones on the grassy bank overlooking the top of the fir trees. Bret would follow the logging road up the side of the mountain until the road petered out to a way trail cutting through the brush. Bret just walked through the saplings. The difference between his path and the surrounding forest was almost imperceptible. He could see the grade cut into the side of the mountain because, at one time, the loggers had hauled rail tracks up this way to cart out the gigantic old trees. At the top, Bret came to a plateau way above the North Fork of the Snoqualmie River, near a stream of black water rushing down from snow fields tucked away in valleys no one ever visited. He stood on the road and listened to the stream. He could hear something in the stream making a noise. *Knock. Knock. Knock.* He found the noisemaker along the side of the stream. A snag lay caught in the stones and, as the water volume jumped a tiny bit and dropped a tiny bit, the caught lumber cracked into a stone and then bounced back, and then it cracked into the stone and bounced back, over and over again. Listening to the articulation of the snow melt and the fallen tree, a sound that would go on endlessly regardless of his being there to hear it, filled Bret with a comfortable feeling, a lack of consequence in the world.

Sometimes he wished he had asked Martha out when he had his chance in second period Biology. Martha had sat in front of him. For three weeks during his sophomore year and her junior year Martha had turned around to talk to him. She smiled, her lips coated in a faint transparent lip gloss, and brushed back her long hair with a hand full of pink polished nails. "What're you doing this weekend?"

Bret thought this was an accusation because he didn't have any plans. Instead of saying, "Nothing, what would you like to do?" he said to prove that he had a life, "Going camping."

"Where?"

"Sunday Lake."

The next Friday when Martha asked, "What're you doing this weekend?"

Bret said, "Going to Spokane."

"Why?"

"To visit my grandparents."

That last Friday, she was late between classes and just before the teacher started, she turned and asked him and he smiled at her and then the class started and he never did say, "Nothing, what would you like to do?"

Martha started dating Russ soon after.

After the accident, the story in school went, "Dude, she was fucking decapitated." Jerry shook his head to acknowledge the horror. "Do you know what that is?"

"Yeah." Bret didn't want to hear anything else.

"It means, dude, her head snapped off her body like she was a fucking doll. When the medics got to the wreck, Russ was, like, holding her head in his lap and stroking her hair and talking to her like he was a toddler. It's amazing he's still as together as he is. Me? Myself? I would go psycho if I killed my old lady in some stupid car wreck."

"He did go psycho. He killed himself." Bret wanted to push past Jerry and keep walking, but when Jerry talked he stood directly in front of his target. Jerry wedged his boots against Bret's tennis shoes. Bret's heels touched the wall. "It wasn't just himself he killed."

"Dude. Sorry. I totally forgot. Sorry."

The sudden attention on top of what he'd done drove Russ over the edge. Just about everyone forgave Russ for being drunk. Dented bumpers and scratched doors picked up during misty and icy drives home scarred most of the trucks and sedans in the valley. Before, everyone would nudge each other when Russ came into the Tift House or the Mar-T Cafe, and they would ignore him because no one wanted to see their kids in North

Bend after they graduated. After this tragedy, Russ became an open symbol of pity rather than an embarrassment. Mothers of kids Russ went to school with now openly approached him and clasped him to their bosoms, opening their arms wide and cradling his head in the crook of their perfumed necks.

Kids drowned swimming in the Snoqualmie almost every summer. The white Search and Rescue van and the fire trucks parked on the bank across from Bret's apartment building. The deputy sheriff motored up and down the river in an aluminum boat, prodding the submerged snags with a long pole. When Russ drowned himself, a steady drizzle fell onto the riling water. A fly fisherman found his bloated, white corpse caught in a snag in the reeds about a half mile above the Snoqualmie Falls.

The day after Bret carried Miss Eaves' basket, he began to wonder what she did out there in the forest where he found her. When he'd passed her she was just standing in the middle of the clearing, swaying back and forth. She didn't even notice he'd come along. It wasn't until he said hello that she turned around to look at him. The basket itself had been too heavy for her to lift. He didn't know how she would have been able to carry it back to the apartment building.

He found Miss Eaves in the hallway. She wore a T-shirt advertising Ron's Gas Station 15 Years of Service, and a pair of paint splattered overalls. Scuffs and nicks scarred the hallway from the tenants that had just moved out. She had a bottle of wood polish, a tin of putty and a thin putty blade and was applying it to the wall. "I hate people moving in and out of this building," she said. "It takes maybe three years for me to begin to know someone and then they leave. How do they expect their next landlord to feel about them? These people rip the carpet when they moved in and they scratch the walls moving out. They leave trash on the sidewalk and when they get to wherever they are going, they'll rip the carpet on the way in and scratch the walls on the way out. Moving is a waste of time for everyone involved."

Bret helped her move the lobby furniture outside. In the sun, the tables looked dingy. Dust and cobwebs clung to the lampshades. Out on the sidewalk everything looked like it was in a yard sale. After they moved everything back inside, Miss Eaves said, "The least I can do is offer you a cup of tea."

"No thanks."

"You have to have some. I have to repay you, somehow. Have you ever experienced mushroom tea before?"

"I haven't."

Bret sat down in a plush chair that had wooden legs with carved balls for feet. The only light came through a stained-glass window, an abstract pattern of white, green and red glass. The jumble of things in her room had a coherence, even though it was stuffed with an assortment of heavy pieces of furniture and layered with framed photographs, bookcases full of books and magazines, a case with yellowed and brown paper sleeves. A thick armoire of heavy wood oiled to a fine sheen with brass handles sat next to the galley kitchen. An arrangement of glass vials and doilies lay on the top of a long chest of drawers. A Tiffany lamp sat next to the chair. The base had a patina of oxidized metal and looked to Bret as if it could use a good polishing. A thick Persian rug with a cigarette burn in the middle covered the wood floor. He watched Miss Eaves in the kitchen. The fiddleheads had been canned and sat in mason jars on the shelf. The mushrooms hung in baskets from the wall.

They waited in silence while the kettle boiled. When it whistled, she stood up and said, "It'll be just a minute." She poured the water through the mushrooms into the tea. "I'm going to put cream and sugar into your drink. Hope you don't mind."

The smell of the damp mushrooms filled her apartment, a forest smell like rotting wood, or snails, or a stepped-on millipede. She wrinkled her nose. "It doesn't taste like this. I sort of like it, but you're probably thinking I'm going to serve you brewed sawdust."

He listened to her open the refrigerator. It burbled and wheezed as she opened the door and poured some thick whipping cream into his cup.

She offered him a plate and a spoon with sugar and salmon berries. They ate these. He sipped his tea, and it tasted like lemon with a twist of potting soil. "This is interesting," he said.

"All stuff I picked up the other day, except the cream."

On a second drink, the earth taste wasn't as strong. He ate the salmon berries. He'd eaten them from the bushes before. They weren't juicy like blueberries, but a bitter berry. With sugar they tasted better.

Bret said, "You know that jacket you bought?" He told her about Martha. Miss Eaves said she was sorry and set her cup down. "Would you like another cup?"

"Sure," he said.

"I knew the story," she said. "I didn't know the names, but I knew that it had happened. I didn't know the boy's name was Skylar. I'm sorry," Miss Eaves said. "You poor dear."

He took the cup from her hand and drank it. She watched him drink, and then she sat down and looked at the stained glass.

"I don't feel well," Bret said after a minute. A slight burning feeling touched his eyes. He felt a heavy numbness creeping through his arms like he couldn't move them. Streaks began to filter down from the light coming through the stained glass, tracers and neon streaks. He stood up and took a step out onto the middle of the Persian rug.

Miss Eaves said, "It's all right."

"I think those mushroom might have been bad. Maybe you should call an ambulance."

He could smell her perfume, the odor of lavender and talcum power and then over that the solvents she used to clean the walls, linseed oil and beeswax. Miss Eaves rocked Bret back onto the chair and took off his shoes. He curled his toes into the plush carpet. He floated inside her room and inside the building and everything had a furry halo around it.

"Do you like the tea?" she asked.

"Did you call an ambulance yet?"

"You like the tea, then." She put a record on, something that sounded like a piano or rain dripping onto asphalt, *tink tink tink tinka tink tink tinka tinka.*

His heart began to beat in time to the music or the dropping water or just the sound. Whatever it was it evened him out. He closed his eyes. Bret wanted to explain the experience of living in his room overlooking the junkyard and looking at the stand of pine trees and Mount Si and the swollen green river because he figured if he understood his own life he would be able to have some control over it. The view out of his window made him feel at once at home and a little depressed. It was something he hadn't realized, but after he returned from his visit to his grandparent's house in Spokane, the first thing he did was open the window and look out there. Bret wanted to explain the view out of his window to Miss Eaves. He described the girder bridge, the flooding emerald Snoqualmie River, the crooked snag tops of the cedar trees on the other bank. The scrap yard leaked rusted red mud into the ditch, and Bret tried to describe the junk, afraid of the mess of detail. When he finished telling her about the view out of his room, his brain felt as if it had been electrified. In describing the junk, he mentally followed the lines of the broken bumpers, the shattered windshields and then the girders of the bridge. His voice had somehow captured all of it in the same, hesitant pitch that he used to say his own name. He told her about the yellow bullet-hole pocked low-clearance sign.

"I didn't know about the sign," Miss Eaves said. "See, I've

lived here all of this time and I didn't know about that." Miss Eaves stood close to him and she smelled like oranges now. The smell reminded him of the fruit stands near his grandparents' house full of apples and plums. His grandmother didn't keep sugar in the house. Bret gorged himself on the fruit, standing in the dusty field between the fruit stand, placing the soft skin of the red plums to his lips and biting and eating and swallowing until he felt faint and his stomach ached. Later his stomach, filled with the golden, overripe plums and apples, felt loose and watery. He'd woken in his bed with his clothes piled on his chair and the taste of dirt on the roof of his mouth.

One winter morning during his senior year, Bret had left algebra with the flu. As he sat next to the radiator, the damp, warm air had started to make his ears ring. He pulled his books to his chest and talked to Mrs. Hacket and she nodded. He walked down the brick hallway, stopping sometimes to look out at the rain falling in sheets on the playfield and the water lying in deep puddles because it couldn't run off the field quickly enough.

He stopped in the locker bay to get his rain jacket and at the other end of the battered metal lockers, under the cold florescent lights, Russ and his Martha were making out. Martha's eyes were closed and her long lashes lay on the smooth rim of her eye socket. Russ had his face pressed up to hers, but he had the back of his head to Bret. So Bret looked at them kissing for maybe longer than he should have. He looked for long enough that Martha opened her eyes and saw him and then she made a slow wink and then closed her eyes again. And Bret put on his rain jacket and suppressed the urge to sneeze and cough and went outside and sneezed and coughed under the flowing gutters in the covered walkway out to the gym. That was the last time Martha saw him.

"They're watching me again," Miss Eaves said.

"Who is watching you again?"

"Get down," she said. "Whisper if you have something to say to me." They crouched under her window. Her hair was loose, and the gray seemed almost like thin strips of neon. The junkyard light came through the window and fell over the chair, and the shadow of the chair and her bed jumped up against the wall.

"There's the man who lives in the junkyard," she said. "And he told me the other day that he has been watching me."

Bret stood up and looked into the junkyard and he couldn't see any activity over at the junkyard.

"You mustn't go out there," she hissed, "or you will never return."

"How do you know you're being watched? Could it just be paranoia?"

"Everyone can tell they're being watched."

Bret crossed the street and walked along the corrugated fence of the junkyard. He didn't see a way in and finally, he climbed up onto the shed and then dropped down into the junkyard. He walked through the junkyard and looked back and saw Miss Eaves' face in her window. "Who's there?" he heard someone say, and then he ran into the junkman. "The junkyard is closed," the junkman said.

"I know," Bret said. "I live in the building across the street. I was sent over here."

"How did you get in?"

He saw the junkman then for the first time without his overalls on. He wore a T-shirt and shorts and leather sandals. His beard was washed and fluffy. It was very white. He looked at Bret, slowly looking up and down. "Why don't you sit down and take a load off?"

"The woman who manages the building across the street,

you'd probably know her if you saw her, she thinks you're watching her."

"Of course I watch her. You'd watch her too if you've seen what I've seen."

"Well, don't watch her."

"What am I supposed to do? I'm sitting here smoking and looking at the river and thinking about things, like a person has a right to do after they have worked all day. I have eyes in my head. She is there in her window, performing, and I figure if she's putting on the show for someone's benefit, it must be mine."

"She told me she saw someone watching her, and I told her I'd do something about it. She didn't seem like she was too happy about it."

"Tell her to close her drapes. Would you like something to drink? Or smoke?"

They sat down under a plexiglass awning on the wide back seat of an old car. The junkman produced a thick, hand-rolled cigarette from his breast pocket and lit it. The end of the paper turned black and fell off, and the weed burned and smelled dark. The junkman puckered and sucked the tip of the joint, winced and handed it to Bret. Bret sucked and then the heavy, bitter smoke burned his lungs. He coughed. The junkman grinned and blew his blue smoke into Bret's face. The place where he sat had some palm trees and ferns and a faint blue light that didn't interfere with the starlight. They looked back at the house, and Bret saw Miss Eaves' light go on and then off.

A pulsing light came from Miss Eaves' room, and he saw her dancing in the window. She wore her slip and rolled her hips slowly. She held her hands over her face and her elbows held high.

"What did I tell you, my friend? Some people want you to help them help themselves. I thought that old bat might be crazy. But you know, I think the true test of a crazy person is that an eccentric person needs an audience, while a crazy person can't help themselves. Whatever is driving them along just keeps going whether they're awake or not or alone or in front of people. I think that broad needs an audience. It's better than being alone," the junkman said. "I don't have an audience and it would be nice. I deal with people all over this valley. I think perhaps I'm the only person who knows the true value of things. How much do you think a can of soda is worth?"

"They cost seventy-five cents in the machine at school."

"A tin can is worth about two cents. The paint on the outside is worth maybe another four cents and let's pay whoever made the art, such as it is, a flat fee and everyone else involved in making that can another penny per can. That's a lot of pennies right? And then how much do you think that soda cost to put in the can? Another penny. So the whole thing, really, is worth two cents empty, and full it's worth about ten cents."

"Why don't you sell your own soda if that's the way it is?"

"I have a mind to," the junkman said. "I have a mind to."

They sat and smoked and finally the curtain fell on Miss Eaves window.

Bret stood up then and stretched. He shook hands with the junkman and as he walked back toward the house, he saw that Miss Eaves' drapes were parted again. Her light was off, and she was staring blankly out at the junkyard. He waved as he came out the front gate. She stared through him, out into the darkness. As he walked back up the stairs to his room, he noticed that someone had closed his door. He opened the door and he could hear someone singing something inside his room.

*Oh where is pretty Polly, Oh yonder she stands;*
*With rings on her fingers, her lily-white hands.*

Miss Eaves rolled out of Bret's bed. She wore Martha's lettermen jacket, but she didn't have anything else on.

Bret closed his door, quickly. "Miss Eaves?"

"No, it's me, Martha. I've been waiting for you Bret. I've always had my eye on you."

Bret's skin felt cold suddenly. He felt the roots of the hair on his arms and his neck and his scalp tingle. She stretched her palms toward the ceiling, like Martha stretched in gym. "What's wrong with you?" he asked. Although his natural inclination was to turn on the light, he didn't. He wanted Miss Eaves to be Martha but the reality of Miss Eaves in his room scared him. Her breath smelled, an organic smell like milk that had been left in the refrigerator long enough that it was beyond sour and had altered into something else. Flecks of hard mucus clung to the edge of her mouth, almost like the flak that gathered around his mouth when he had been running for a long time. "Can I get you glass of water?"

"I never died, Bret," she said. She sat down on the edge of the bed. Her toes kicked back and forth under the bed. "It was just some crazy story my parents devised, so that they could send me to college and start out fresh without Russ following me. They didn't think he'd kill himself."

"Yeah?" Bret asked. "Are you thirsty, Miss Eaves?"

"Martha," she said.

"Are you thirsty?"

"Yes."

"Is water all right?"

"Water is grand," she said. He poured her a glass of water. The water sung and rose in pitch as it filled the glass. Bret opened the door to his room and looked down the hallway. The junkyard light fell through the even spaces of the windows against the carpeted floor. He sat down on the bed next to Miss Eaves and handed her the glass.

"Why did you come back?"

"I missed you," she said.

"You didn't even know me."

"Do you know how sometimes you have that connection with someone? You may have only seen them once but they're someone you think about all of the time. When I saw you, it was like this. I thought about you all of the time. And I always thought I would one day see you. That I would one day be with you."

He wanted to believe she was Martha as much as Miss Eaves wanted to believe that she was Martha. She lay back on the bed and the old letterman's jacket opened up. The blue light from the junkyard across the street fell through the drapes. Her breasts rolled into two flattened mounds. He didn't know how to get her out of his room, so he left. He walked outside. Across the street, he could see the embers of the junkman's joint.

Later that summer, when the corn stalks were almost six feet tall, Bret woke one night to the sound of someone playing a song. It was a woman singing, and then it stopped, and then he heard it again, a sound knocked around by the wind. He looked out of his window, but just saw the dark junkyard and the black river glittering where the water parted around the snags. Bret put on his sweat pants and tennis shoes and went down the steps outside and then walked around the building at the edge of the field. He could hear the music coming from inside the corn. He found a place where a row had been pushed over, so he walked along there and then down the long, rustling hallway of stalks. He came to a slight knoll where the farm machines couldn't run, so there wasn't any corn. There was a gigantic black cherry tree there hanging with fruit. He could smell the warm fruit, and he heard the birds gorging themselves.

Miss Eaves had spread a blanket next to a portable stereo playing old songs. She wore a crown of burning candles. When she turned around and saw Bret there, she laughed. The birds were the size of monkeys hanging in the tree.

"I don't think this hat is helping me any, but I like it anyway. How do I look?"

Her face was in the shadows of the crown. She wore the jacket and a nightgown. Wax splattered on her shoulders. Again he thought she looked as if she was even his age, just out of high school.

"Wonderful," Bret said. They were in their own place. The long grass around the heavy trunk of the cherry tree was trampled.

"Help yourself to some coffee. I brought two cups in case anyone came out here looking for me."

"Thank you." He poured himself some coffee out of the tin coffee pot.

"Help yourself to some brownies."

"Thank you." He helped himself to some brownies.

"When you're done drinking my coffee and eating my brownies, can I ask you a favor?"

The violin wailed through the verse.

"Sure," Bret said.

"Climb into the tree and tell me what you can see."

"All right."

"Thank you," she said. He could see her liver-spotted neck in the wide arc of the T-shirt collar ending in the smooth skin over her collar bone. Wax from the candles dripped and splattered on her jeans. Red wax encased her fingers.

The buttery brownies dissolved in his mouth and then he swallowed the creamy, sweet coffee. He picked some of the cherries from the tree and ate those. All around them, it was just the corn and then the stars faintly visible above the halo of light coming from her hat. The stars were solid and permanent in the sky. The same constellations sparkled there as on the night Bret's father and Bret had watched a gigantic meteor shower. The meteors themselves fell into the atmosphere, usually looking just like any other star, except they moved through the other stars and then just faded away. Dozens of them appeared and disappeared. Occasionally, one left a long trail that took a while to fade.

"If you're finished eating, could you do the sensible thing and get in the tree?" Miss Eaves said.

Bret grabbed the tree. Long strips of bark peeled away from the tree where the bark had started to shed. The scabrous bark leaked black pitch.

"Oh yes," she said him. "Take off your clothes, first."

Bret looked around, and it was just him and Miss Eaves and the ears of corn rustling a little in the breeze coming down from the pass. He took off his clothes and folded them into a neat bundle and placed them on the blanket. The earth felt cool on the naked soles of his feet. He climbed up into the tree, and the crows and seagulls started to screech and then they took off. Miss Eaves muttered from the ground. "Yes. Yes, that's good." Bret found a comfortable spot and stood there and then waited. From up there, he could see her and the waving tops of the corn, and then the road and the apartment building and the cluster of brick buildings by the bridge and the river running along and the world felt finite and perfect, and he and Miss Eaves were the only people awake and doing anything.

In September, the combine harvesters ran all day. They kicked up huge clouds of dust and chaff and spewed the corn into the back of mammoth trailers. Bret only half paid attention to them, because for him they meant the beginning of football season and the start to the bad weather, and he usually went hiking more to get the most out of the last good days. He didn't see Miss Eaves.

The morning after climbing in the cherry tree, Bret ran into his friend, Jerry, buying some bottled water and a scone at the Milk Barn. Bret didn't recognize him at first in his tight silver, racing shorts and the smooth muscular curve of his skinny legs. Jerry smiled. "Bret?"

"Hey, Jerry," Bret said. Bret had assumed he was just another one of the bicyclists that crowded the old Sunset Highway across the valley during the weekend. They drove their BMW's, Acuras, and Mercedes to the Park and Ride in North Bend. The whole place was so full of cars with bike racks that people who had anywhere to actually go on the bus had to park on the street or just drive to town on the weekend. Bret had a vague idea of what these people did for a living, some job in Bellevue in one of the office parks with white concrete and mirror glass and the parking lots full of these same cars.

Jerry held his helmet under his arm like a casserole bowl. "Do you still live out here, or are you just visiting your folks?"

"I live in the same place."

Bret saw that Jerry remembered that Bret didn't have any folks. Jerry blushed and then murmured, "Well, that's great, you still live in the same old place." He flipped his helmet on and rode away on his bicycle to catch up with the other cyclists he had been with. Bret had seen those bikes at a store in Redmond. He had gone there to trade some books at the Paperback Exchange and he wanted to look for a good bike to get to work on. 850 dollars. His Toyota Celica had only cost 600 dollars. Sure, it was a stick and already old when be bought it, but those bikes cost more than his car.

It hadn't frosted yet, even though a fog clung to the river and drifted over the field. Bret put on his boots and walked out in the field. The stalks had been sawed off just above the ground and, as he walked through the foggy field, it was like the entire planet was just those gnawed corn stalks. The fog felt cool against his face and water started to drip from his hair. He came finally to the cherry tree out in the middle of the field. There were still cherry pits in the crushed soil around the tree, but everything around the tree was barren. The sun came over Mount Si then, a gigantic red disc shining through the fog. Bret pulled himself up in the tree and watched the fog start to drift away in the sunlight. A crow landed on one of the upper branches and flipped its head one way and then the other to look Bret over and then it flew off when Bret didn't have anything to offer.

A week after Bret had climbed the tree, he heard from the junkman that something had happened to Miss Eaves. She had been found wandering in her nightgown without any shoes on one of the Weyerhaeuser access roads. She didn't remember where she was, so the security guard took her to the King County Sheriff's office in North Bend and they took her to the Snoqualmie Medical Center. She didn't know what had happened to her. She was sitting in her apartment and then suddenly got the urge to go for a walk. She said she was just out for a walk to let off some steam. She didn't know where she was headed.

"Anything could've happened to that crazy old woman," the junkman said. He wore greasy overalls and stood on the cement block by the front door and threw his cigarette butts into an old Hills Brothers can full of cat litter.

Bret didn't see Miss Eaves for a week. He went about his life and when finally he saw her, she was sweeping cobwebs out of the stairwell, and he was rushing because he was late for work. She stopped when Bret came down the stairs. "Hello," she said, and then she went back to sweeping.

"Hi, Miss Eaves," Bret said.

She stopped sweeping and leaned on her broom. "Even sweeping can be hard work when you get to be my age."

Skin as coarse and brown as old corn stalks covered her sharp elbows. Miss Eaves had lost a lot of weight and now she was stooped and small. He reached to embrace her. She cowered away from Bret and then smiled at him as if he had said something that reminded her of something, and then her face went blank again.

"I can help," Bret said.

She handed him the broom.

"Not now," he said. "But I can help when I get home from work."

"It needs to be done right now," she said.

"Well, let me know and I can help," he said. "And if you need me to carry your basket, I can do that, too," he said.

She looked at Bret and cupped his face in her hands. "You lovely boy. If you knew the places I'd been. I found her, though. I found her for you."

"Who?"

"Martha."

"Martha is dead, Miss Eaves."

"She isn't. I found her for you."

Soon after, Miss Eaves was missing and then she was down-river, with a cord of electrical wire tied around her ankles and a crown of coat-hangers on her head. Bret stood on the clay banks of the Snoqualmie River, looking into the green, riling water. The current carried a record of the clay and soil along the river's path down from the mountains. Deadfalls and ancient stumps as large as houses lay in the river collecting reeds and stray branches in their worn knots and limbs. The whole river smelled familiar. He'd grown up in the odor of silt and water and mold.

When the county buried Miss Eaves in the cemetery on the old Sunset Highway, only a couple of tenants from the building stood there, in blazers and jeans, in dark blue dresses, under umbrellas that did nothing to prevent the drizzle from permeating their clothes. The junkman walked with Bret back to the building. He grabbed him by the back of the neck and said, "Dude, I won't say a word about what I've seen."

Bret looked at him. "What have you seen?"

"Do you think I'm blind?"

Before they came into her room to clear it out, Bret checked the door. The bolt snapped and he pulled the door back and stepped into her room. The lettermen's jacket hung on the back of a chair. It felt heavier than he remembered. Their fathers were proud of their sons' jackets, justifying the expense because they had worn them for so many years themselves after high school. Bret's dad had been proud of his. After graduation, the jackets ended up in childhood closets along with their Little League trophies and yearbooks. The Antique Barn was full of lettermen's jackets, decades worth of discarded coats from parents getting rid of things before retiring to Tucson. Bret thought it odd that they sold these things, but then they must have had houses full of equally sentimental knickknacks. The Antique Barn kept a back room full of musty annuals dating all of the way back to the '40s. Jackets, discontinued uniforms, the Pepto-Bismol-pink single-piece grade school desks, all this junk gathering a layer of mold under the old barn roof before it passed on to the county dump. As lives passed out of the valley, they left behind empty rooms and empty clothes, and thrift stores full of odds and ends and cemeteries packed with plots. The cemetery had expanded over the decades into the neighboring farms, but because the graves lay on the hundred-year flood plain, the city was talking about moving the graveyard up onto the hillside under the new housing development. Last spring, the flood had reached right up to the edge of the cemetery and when it receded, dozens of graves had turned into sink holes.

Bret put the jacket on. His fingers slid down the silky sleeves. The jacket was way too small. It pulled taut over his forearms and across his shoulder blades. He walked around Miss Eaves' room with the jacket on. He noticed the light falling in from the junkyard and the paintings on the wall of all of the things she had seen and tried to translate into something that would outlast her. Paintings covered the walls and the ceiling and lay in stacks on the floor. Decades of careful work. He thought about which one he might take and finally he left them. He found her battered tackle box and the heavy tin full of oil paint tubes. He lifted the bundle of brushes as heavy as a block of firewood. He removed the jacket. The tight sleeves had cut off his circulation until his hands tingled. He took off the jacket and left with her painting supplies.

The spring came, and the farmer had his tractor out in the field and was planting the corn. The flood filled half the field and then it receded, and up on the hills around Snoqualmie, more houses were built. Bret had the urge to leave the building and his view of the junkyard. He figured the benefit of knowing how to wash dishes was that they've got dirty dishes just about everywhere. But anywhere Bret went, he'd still be surrounded by the absence of people no longer with him. He remained in Snoqualmie. He drew a picture of the wrecked car and the Snoqualmie River as the hair of the girl he had never asked what she was doing next weekend and would she like to do something with him? Miss Eaves floated over the river, hanging from the talons of a larger-than-life crow. His parents lay in a tangle of roots under the cherry tree. He found himself naked in the cherry tree with a wire crown of candles dripping hot red wax on his shoulders. He found himself swimming in the dark while the stars melted underwater like sugar, and in the cold, his heart slowed to a murmur.